AFROBEAT

Editor Patsy Antoine
Cover Random Design
Inside pages design Essuman & Gehrig
Distributed by Central Books 0181 986 4854
Website www.pulpfact.demon.co.uk
Thanks to The Arts Council of England, London Arts Board, and all the writers who sent their work in.

First published 1999 by Pulp Faction
© in this collection 1999, Pulp Faction
All rights reserved,
including the right to reproduce
this book or portions thereof
in any form whatsoever.
Permission must be obtained for the
reproduction of any item.
Printed in England.
ISBN: 1899571086

Contents

Glow **Roger Robinson** 4
The Roaring Man **Judith Bryan** 13
True Love **Patricia Cumper** 21
The Great White Hate **Courttia Newland** 29
Joy **Patsy Antoine** 39
Johnny Can Sleep Easy Now **JJ Amoworo Wilson** 45
The Car **Lucas Loblack** 51
Who Am I? **Natalie Stewart** 61
The Price Of Maybe **Kadija Sesay** 65
White Walls **Deborah Ricketts** 75
Trust Me **Brenda Emmanus** 77
Crates **Joanna Traynor** 87
A Good Buy **Yinka Sunmonu** 97
The Negative **Norma Pollock** 107
A SuitableCandidate **Norma Pollock** 113
Author Notes 123

Glow
Roger Robinson

So, there I was in the club. My arms wrapped around Charmaine's supple body. She was the object of a childhood crush that had gained strength exponentially as I'd grown into adulthood, so when she returned that summer from a lengthy stay in America, her status had gone from adolescent town beauty to that of triumphant queen-like goddess.

The rest of the guys were sipping multi-coloured cocktails and gave me the thumbs up every time I glanced in their direction. I knew each one of them wished they were in my position. You see in Ilford, nothing much happens. Well, not to us anyway. That's why I felt so good about Charmaine's body pressed tightly against mine, as the slow tunes serenaded us under ultraviolet light. With every dance we pressed harder and harder, holding on to each other through even the upbeat rare groove selection, till the slow tunes came around.

Then, quite suddenly, my stomach convulsed with the most painful of cramps. Nerves. It had to be. I made an excuse that I needed the toilet and once safely in the confines of the gent's, looked at myself in the toilet mirror, staring into my own dark brown eyes, trying to regain my composure. I splashed water on my face, took a few deep breaths and the cramps settled.

I walked confidently out of the toilet, and immediately noticed people staring at my genital area. I reached down instinctively, thinking my pants were unzipped, but the zip was shut tight. When I looked down to see what everyone was staring at, there it was. My dick was glowing, fluorescent green in the dark of the club. Lying still in quiet repose like a small plutonium rod or a very, very small *Star Wars* light sabre. It was glowing right through the dark denim jeans I was wearing and everyone could see it. I stared at it for a few seconds completely flabbergasted, then looked up at the growing crowd around me staring at it. As they looked in my eyes with the unspoken what's going on down there, then? emblazoned across their faces, it slowly dawned on me that they could see its exact size and shape.

'Oh my God! What if Charmaine sees it in its resting state and thinks it's really small,' I thought to myself. 'Worse yet, what if she sees it...'

I took off my leather jacket and tied it around my waist to cover it up, went straight up to Charmaine and with a hasty goodbye said that I'd call her soon. I didn't have time to explain to the guys.

I drove home wondering what the hell was happening to me. At every red traffic light I lifted the leather jacket to see if it was still glowing. Just before I checked each time I'd pray it was gone but there it was glowing ever brighter, adding a green tint to the dark interior of the car, causing oncoming drivers to look over as they passed me by.

I got home, took off the jacket and turned the lights on and off for ten minutes straight, hoping that somehow the glow would turn itself off. Frustrated and confused I went to bed staring at it in the dead centre of my sheet, glowing straight through like a green beacon.

Next morning I woke up to the sound of a ringing phone. It was Jake asking me what the hell had happened, and how come I'd just run out on Charmaine when things were looking so good. I lied and told him I wasn't feeling very well, which wasn't exactly a lie, unless you considered fluorescent green privates a sign of good health.

He said that after I'd left she'd come across to Jake and the guys, almost in tears, asking them why I left so suddenly. Asking them if I already had a girlfriend, and saying that the only real reason she'd come back was to see if things could work with me.

'Do you still like her?'

'Of course I do, Jake.'

'Well you better call her then because every guy I know is gearing up to make a move on her since they heard that you just up and left her in the club. Give her a call now.' He rung off.

More stressed than ever I picked up the phone to dial her number. Then I thought what am I doing? What the hell would I tell her? Come across to my flat for a candlelit dinner and, uhm, by the way, just ignore the fact that my member's glowing flurorescent green...

I laid the phone gently back in its receiver.

Three days passed and I was still fluorescent. I didn't leave the house and I didn't call Charmaine or anyone else. Then on Thursday the phone rang at about noon while I was in the toilet. I came out to hear Charmaine's exasperated voice.

'I thought you were going to call me? Have I done something to upset you? Please give me a call, I just want to talk.'

I listened in complete turmoil, not even daring to pick up the phone. This predicament was too embarrassing to explain.

The phone rang again and I let the answer machine get it. It was Jake.

'Hi, Dwayne, me and the guys are coming over tomorrow to check up on you and...'

I picked up.

'Hi, Jake.'

'Oh you're there. Are you screening your calls now?'

'No, I was just in the toilet,' I half-lied.

'Are you alright man? You've been acting pretty weird. Why haven't you been out your house, and why didn't you call Charmaine for God's sake?'

'I've got a lot on my mind right now...'

'Anyway me and the guys are coming over to check up on you,' and before I could argue otherwise he hung up the phone.

I started to panic. I didn't know what to do. I couldn't let the guys see me glowing. How would I explain it? Then I had an idea. No one would know that my dick was fluorescent green if I wore trousers exactly the same colour, or leather underwear to stop it from glowing through my clothes...

So I rang up an Ann Summers sex shop.

'Hi, do you have leather underwear?' I asked.

'Yes we do, sir.'

'...and fluorescent green pants?'

'Yes, but only in 50 per cent Lycra, stretch-to-fit leggings,' came the efficient response.

'Do you deliver?'

'Yes, sir, we do.'

'Great!' I read out the digits on my Amex card and paid extra for their 24-hour delivery service.

The next day I woke up praying my package would be delivered before Jake and the rest of the guys arrived. Minutes before they'd said they'd be over the bell rang. It was the sex shop courier.

'A delivery of leather underwear and fluorescent green 50 per cent Lycra pants for a Dwayne Powell. Could you sign here, please? And here's a copy of our free complementary brochure for new customers...'

'Thank you.'

I closed the door and slipped quickly into my new pants. It worked. Not even a hint of the glow was visible. The only problem was they were a bit figure-hugging and the high Lycra content gave them a slight sheen...

Then the bell rang. It was the guys. I opened the door, to see them with pizzas and six-packs in their hands. They stood staring at me from head to toe, from my grey flannel hoodie to my figure-hugging fluorescent green pants and my Air Jordans. They stared silently, with faces twisted into quizzical concern. I told them to come in. They sat and popped a few beers and made nervous small talk between themselves.

Then Jake burst out, 'I can't take this anymore. Dwayne, the guys and me have something to ask you. Are you gay?'

I nearly choked on my triangle of pizza. 'What the hell would make you think that?'

'Well, firstly, you bluntly refuse to sleep with Charmaine and that, combined with your new more extreme fashion sense, and the unopened leather underwear on the floor...' he trailed off.

I paused for a moment, seeing his point completely, and all the guys froze, too as they waited for my reply.

Then Jake says, 'Well are you? Are you gay? Because if you are it'd still be cool...'

'No, I'm not gay.'

They let out a collective sigh of relief.

'Then what's going on with you?' he persisted.

'Look, man, I know it looks weird but I can't explain what's going on right now,' I said.

Then I told them they had to go.

'Can we at least finish the beers and the pizza?'

'No. Everyone's got to go now, I don't feel well.'

As I ushered them out their faces wore expressions more confused than when they'd arrived. I closed the door and threw myself on the bed in complete frustration. Then the door buzzed again.

'Who is it?'

'It's Charmaine. If you don't let me in right now and make love to me. I'm going to book myself on the first ticket back to New York tomorrow.'

I couldn't let her leave. I opened the door and she walked in confidently and sat on the couch.

I sat next to her and she held my hand, burst into tears and said, 'What's going on? I come all this way to be with you and you can't even make a simple phone call? I just saw the guys on my way here and they said I shouldn't waste my time because you're gay. Is it true?'

'No, those guys don't know anything,' I said quickly.

'Then prove it to me,' she said as she leaned forward and began kissing me.

Overcome by her beauty, I kissed her back, passionately. She peeled off my grey flannel hoodie and she slid out of her top. Her handfuls of pert breast hypnotised me. I kissed them gently almost forgetting my fluorescent situation. She tried to pull down my pants and suddenly I remembered. My predicament came flooding back.

I said, 'Wait! Before you do that, I have something to tell you.'

She pressed her fingers to my lips and said, 'You wait. I have something to show you first...' She took two steps back and began to unbutton the jeans of her lady-cut Levi's and fluorescent green rays shot from her crotch like laser beams.

10

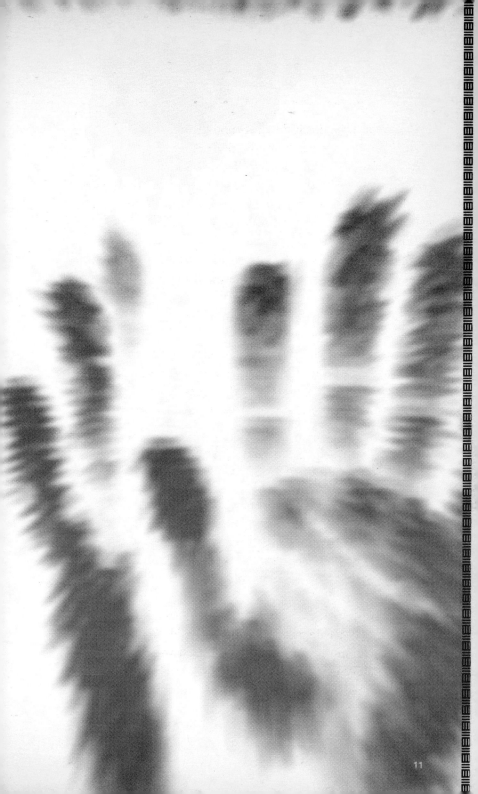

The Roaring Man
Judith Bryan

He wears a good, grey suit. He takes the train to work. He sits in the window, every morning, every evening. The train waits a frantic three minutes at each station. Careless of whispers and the empty seat beside him in the rush hour, he wrings the space between his hands. From the platform, he is behind glass, behind the babble of boarding and alighting. He only seems silent. What barks and howls emit from his stretching mouth? Whose murder does he enact, twice daily, for all to see?

At home, he has a wife. She is so brittle it hurts her to breathe. She is flailing in the depths, failing by slow degrees to keep her head above water. All of her days are grey or rainy. When they are both she stands beside the window, holding the thin grimed stuff of the net curtain between two fingers, staring at rain making long puddles on the tarmac. The light from the houses and the fractured glow of the street lamps adds something almost like colour to the patchwork of water and road. Then it is time for her husband to come home, and she leaves the window. The nets fall slowly, slowly, whisper promises or obscenities. She has a secret and, finally, she must tell him.

He greets the news with a face as hard and unforgiving as a lake in winter. He says, 'Is it mine?' and turns away without waiting for an answer. He never was a talkative man, at least not to her. Now, in the privacy of their own home, he reserves his conversations for himself. He mutters behind his fingers, sputters his fury against the knuckles of his clenched fist; and turns away from her. Now their house is full of words, sibilant eddies of sound stirring the still air.

She confides in her mother. Mother says he is only worried: about finances, and his job security, and the need to build a bright future, now he is to be a family man. But then, she calls her daughter's somnolence 'the calm bloom of pregnancy', and reads her frozen smile as happiness. 'The best years of your life are now unfolding,' she says. 'Marriage. Motherhood.' Mother pats her arm, brushes the hair from her eyes. 'Dear child, you really are a woman now.' And they shed a tear or two together, but for different reasons.

The roaring man's wife is a disembodied head; a death mask caught up in a masquerade. She is whirling down a long, brightly-lit street, festooned with ribbons and lanterns, while beneath her feet the ground is hard and dark and dry as bones. It reaches on and on into the night, and she can see where the lights run out, where the people fade back into the bush. There she will have to dance alone with nothing to keep her feet in rhythm but a dim memory of someone else's celebration.

She has never felt more full of echoes.

The days pass. He performs his tasks. He makes his way home.

The train begins its journey from the station where he gets on and there is always a seat by the window for him. He watches the dark draw in across the afternoon sky, running fast streaks of colour behind telephone wires and over railway cables. Parallel lines rise and fall, rush to meet then pull away, until the sky is all black, but for the orange eyes of neon lamps. Then his hands begin to talk with their own eloquent will. But his mouth, tired from a day of utterances, keeps counsel. Is it better this way?

He returns to their house and is greeted by the sighs of her movement, the incantation of her steps, the rhythmic pulse of her breathing, low and shallow, rasping, whispering, always whispering. She bends her head so her hair falls fine and damp across her face. She tries to hide from him the ceaseless movement of her lips. Even behind closed eyelids, he sees those thin white lips rise and fall, rush to meet, then pull away. Pouring rapid curses, spells, blasphemies. Piling them high into the void between them. It is she who is building the wall. Not him.

Tonight, from behind the kitchen door, he can hear a radio playing some crap about god and the essence of the sacred. Over the muffled words comes the intermittent rattle of cutlery against wood and china. She is making supper, coughing softly, rustling her long dress across the floor, reciting the names of food as she touches and strokes and licks each item. He cannot go in there. He cannot go into that room where his wife makes love to vegetables and kitchen utensils with more pride and passion than she has ever shown him. Still he is drawn to her. The rising scent of her, squeezing through the walls, pulls him nearer. Until he stands before the closed door, his hands tracing its height and width. He can tell she is there on the other side. She is waiting for him, willing him to come and bear witness.

He'll be damned if he lets her win.

As she leaves the kitchen to lay the table for their meal, he is there, in front of her. They are so near his breath lifts the downy hair of her fringe. She sees his face, full before her like a revelation. All the muscles twisting and working, moving like pistons. His eyes colourless as glass, his skin a furious red. He seems to her like a mirror, perfect reflection; for even as his lips move, so do hers. He is her voice and she is his. They draw together like pus in a sore. His hands tremble as they move over her body. He finds her nipples and pulls and squeezes. He watches the shock pass over her face, but his is as lacking in curiosity as a sleepwalker. His fingers run over her belly, seeking, for the first time, evidence of her metamorphosis. She hears herself entreat him, like a new bride in a pre-war melodrama, 'Be gentle with me,' before they fall. They catch the tablecloth as they descend. They lie amongst the cutlery and broken plates, and merge for the last time.

She had thought they might be closer then. Things might be better. But she has been waiting at milestones for a long time. The wedding, the house; this new life, something they have made between them, together, after all... At each point she has thought 'now' and waited for things to alter. Still, they remain merely themselves, each occupying their allotted space, moving in small circles. Stopping occasionally to gaze, with some dismay, at one another. Then she thought: more grey days. Darker and ever more dreary, lighter on the surface only as they move through summer toward the next milestone, the next change that isn't a change. How strange it feels to be wrong.

She is smooth and taut, a slow rising helium balloon. She fills and deflates, fattens and mutates, each day altering in unexpected ways. This evolution is not linear and she is taken by surprise. She dreams about the baby. In her dream she is in the bathroom at her mother's house, struggling to untangle the retractable washing line over the bath. The cords are a mass of twine. The whole thing threatens to slip its moorings. She is perplexed but patient. One by one, she unravels the lines, stretching to complete her task. Her belly hangs low and ponderous over the bath tub. The baby moves against taut muscles, rippling like water over stones, then stronger, like the stones themselves, rolling and gathering.

She is sitting on the edge of the bath, line restored above her head. She watches the patterns in the tiles and waits for the baby to move again. There. A tentative scraping, little cat scratch, and a thin angle of skin appears beside her belly button. Back and forth it moves. A knee, or perhaps an elbow, nudging her, inviting intrigue. Then come five tiny fingers, webbed inside the fine mesh of her skin. The hand closes to a fist that moves through her skin without breaking the surface. She reaches down, uncurls the little fingers with her own.

The baby's face is in the pattern in the tiles. Her own face is there too. Their images drift and alter like flames, making new shapes. They are all colours green: apple and avocado, leaf and lime, and she thinks of a meadow, or of rice shoots in a paddy field, and she holds the baby's hand and she laughs.

Her laughter echoes in her ears and she wakes up. Her face is wet with tears. She can't remember the end of her dream. She has the nagging thought that, if she really laughed that hard, she would have fallen backwards into the bath.

Yes, it is best that his tongue refrain from telling its version and leaves the story to his hands. They tell the tale with subtlety, rarely rising more than a few inches from his lap or his sides. They flutter and clasp, smooth the air before them, dance there, clench and come to rest. They cannot hiss or roar loud enough to startle even himself, leaving him surrounded by suspicious disapproving glances.

At work both hands and mouth do only what is required of them. They speak of deadlines. Priorities, performance and profits. He is in control. He is here and now, not there, with his wife and her 'tumour'. But in his times of rest, journeying to work and coming back; waiting for his wife to serve the supper; lying beside her in the bed, hearing her shallow breathing then, is there anything he could not do? He feels molten power course through him. It moves along the tributaries of his veins. He pulsates with energy. He waits to be released.

The baby he calls her tumour grows. In the mornings she stands and yawns, loud and wide, moving her arms in circles over her head. Weak sunlight glints over the curves of her breasts and shuns the deep valley between them.

He watches her from the bed. She needn't bother with her full-length cotton gowns, mock Puritan in her tucks and sleeves. Mock modest. Against the bright square of the windowpane all of her roundness is exposed. Over-ripe, she sways when she walks. Her movements are languorous and her glance is sly. She spends long minutes in the bathroom, far longer than it used to take to run his morning bath. Oils and unguents appear in the bathroom cabinet, and he sees the bottles slowly empty and notes the changing smells of her skin. He knows what she becomes behind closed doors, away from his eyes. He knows how she touches herself, as only a lover should, as she has never allowed him to. And this is why she smiles to herself from behind her hair, and why her whispering now sounds like a lullaby, or the wind in high trees. So soft he could almost believe in her. So low he could almost fall under her spell.

Lately, she has become afraid. She has noticed that they are no longer the same reflections in a sallow glass. As she blooms, so he seems to creep in on himself. As she grows calm and slow, he becomes more agitated. She catches him clawing the air, snatching at nothing like a baited bear. And whilst she sings new songs to their little child, he moans, low and bitter, behind gritted teeth. At night she lies awake, listening to him listening to her not sleeping. Some mornings, she feels the imprint of his hands around her throat.

True Love
Patricia Cumper

Robert realised that it must have been love at first sight. At the time he hadn't paid much attention to the tingling in the pit of his stomach, or the slight sweatiness of his palms. He just remembered an urgent desire to get closer to her, to touch her, to have her respond to his commands.

The morning after he drove her home, he came wide awake almost immediately. For a moment, he lay looking at his wife's plump, slack face as she slept beside him. In the dawn light that crept in through the shutters, he could see that the curls of her hair were streaked with grey. Even though the morning was still cool, she was perspiring slightly. His eyes strayed to the bedside table, to where the keys lay gleaming. Slipping quietly out of bed, he held them in his hand, smooth against his palm. The urge to get away from his wife and to be with her became overwhelming.

'Just going for a quick run, love,' he whispered to his wife as she opened one sleepy eye. She smiled and went easily back to sleep.

He never did go running. Instead he drove through the suburban avenues, confined by their orderly hedges of bougainvillea and hibiscus, towards New Kingston where, with its wide streets and gleaming, empty office blocks, they could be alone together. Only when he saw the bare-footed cleaners start sweeping the streets and the primary school children in their starched and faded school uniforms gathering at the bus stops, did Robert reluctantly turn for home.

Soon he went out every morning. He noticed how differently people treated him when they were together, how respectfully his colleagues greeted him. He drove more aggressively, sat more upright at the wheel, felt more commanding than he ever had before. Everyone said how much better he was looking: how healthy, how clear of eye, how much his posture had improved. Robert knew it had been love, pure and uncomplicated. Needing no words, allowing no doubt.

It had begun innocently enough with a tip from a friend who owed him a favour. Jamaica Agribusiness Consortium is going to go public, he had said. When they do, buy as many shares as you can get your hands on. Robert had made a handsome profit as the value of his shares soared. It was a colleague who jokingly suggested at the annual Senior Executive luncheon, that it was time he owned a classic Benz. Robert already had the well-bred, brown-skinned wife, two children attending the schools for which they'd been registered as soon as they were conceived, and the pink and white house that overlooked Kingston from the foothills. The car would be more than a status symbol: it would be a shrewd investment. It would show his colleagues and competitors that he was a successful member of Kingston's new, black corporate elite. He'd placed the order for the Benz the next day.

Robert had had no idea how much he would enjoy the softness of her leather seats, her responsiveness when he stepped on the accelerator, the respect the three-pointed star on her hood commanded from both rich and poor. Her lines, even after thirty years, were aristocratic and her weight and power assured him that he was in command of the best Europe had to offer.

Robert took to turning the air conditioning on full blast and wearing Ralph Lauren suits to the office, despite the heat, so that he would look as elegant as she did. He carried large amounts of change to pay the hordes of ragged boys who charged the car at the traffic lights not to wipe her windscreen with their grubby window cleaners. As Robert left the office each evening, he checked to see that she'd been properly washed and polished, and wiped away any smeared fingerprints with his handkerchief. He was proud that the attendants at the gas station knew to immediately wash off any drops of gas that dripped from the hose and to clean the dip stick with fresh rags. He tipped them generously. Sometimes he would just stand and look at her.

For a while, Robert had volunteered to take the children to school so he could spend even more time on the road. But then small things began to irritate him. His son always cleaned his Air Nikes in the car leaving small deposits of dust and grit on the carpet. His daughter, desperate to control roots that Robert noticed were as coarse as his own, fussed continuously with her hair, often leaving her comb and a tangle of broken strands on the back seat. His wife was, however, happy to resume dropping the children to school in her estate when Robert bribed her with a year's deluxe membership at the Liguanea Club. As the pounds began to drop away, people commented that she, too, was looking much better.

At the office, he felt confined by the corporation's specially-commissioned carpeting and the matching Ken Spencer seascape on his wall. His hands longed for the feel of her wheel and his dedication, once the talk of the office, was whittled away by anxious thoughts: was someone in the car park leaning on her? Did she need more oil? Should he invest in a new mobile phone, one that would match her interior?

The first time Robert noticed anything about her that he could even begin to criticise was as he sat at a busy New Kingston traffic light. He became aware of the car beside him only gradually, thinking it one of those overdressed Hondas that were so common on the street. But it was another Benz, just like his, vulgar as any whore. There were half a dozen high-level brake lights mounted around the rear windscreen, personalised license plates were set in holders made to look like heavy gold chains and a tacky spoiler ruined the lines of the boot. The whole car vibrated to the driving beat of Dancehall music. Gold teeth glittered in the driver's smile, a smile that suggested that he, as another black man behind the wheel of a Mercedes Benz, was Robert's equal. The flash of anger that exploded in Robert's gut brought sweat to his brow, despite the air conditioning.

He began to notice other small faults. The engine he'd thought sounded like the purr of a contented cat began to sound almost flatulent. The steering felt heavy, unresponsive, and his mechanic, the only other man allowed to touch the Benz, started to talk about having to open up the engine and change all the gaskets and seals. The thought of her so exposed, so vulnerable shook him to his core. He felt humiliated at having to watch her stand with her bonnet open in the middle of the oil-spattered auto repair yard. His heart only slowed from its panicky staccato beat when he climbed back into the car and the coolness from the air conditioning washed over him. He felt the world gradually right itself, and once again he enjoyed the feel of the road beneath her wheels. I'll get a second opinion, Robert thought to himself, as he drove through a city bleached pale by the heat of the dry season: maybe fly someone in from Miami to look at her.

The steady beat of her engine reassured him as he swung wide to avoid a tired Austin Cambridge, and raced up the steep hill road towards home. There was nothing wrong with her, Robert decided, nothing that fixing up her appearance wouldn't put right.

He considered having her re-sprayed in a colour that would set off her lines better than the deep blue she now wore. He thought about red for a while, but finally settled on a metallic grey that, if you looked closely, (as Robert often did) had small flecks of silver in it.

A few months later, at the beginning of the rainy season, the Benz let him down. No warning, no sign of discontent: she didn't care about the agony of embarrassment she was causing him in the middle of evening rush-hour traffic. She simply stopped and refused to start again. As he sat there, bewildered, the rain began to fall. Large, splashing drops flattened on her windscreen and dripped slowly downwards. Her wipers wouldn't move, she wouldn't respond in any way: just those drops winding slowly down the windscreen, like tears. For a moment he convinced himself that she was just doing this to get his attention. He turned the key again, confident she would start, sure that he had understood her motives. She was unresponsive: not a cough, not a flutter, not a sound. As the coolness of the air conditioning faded, he cradled his head in his arms and rested on her steering wheel, deafened by the roar of the rain beating on her roof.

The heat had begun to change the scent of her leather upholstery. It smelt a little like old shoes. Sweat ran down his brow to the end of his nose and splashed onto the mat at his feet. As the rain eased, Robert's sadness gave way first to irritation and then to cold rage. He sat up and reached for his mobile phone. He watched without emotion when the tow truck arrived and hooked the Benz up. Even when he knew the mechanic would fiddle around inside her engine with his grimy hands, he felt nothing.

Because top-of-the-line European cars were rare in Jamaica, it took less than a week to find a buyer. Robert looked pityingly at the line of young middle managers who came and admired her. They peered longingly at her through the rain as she stood seductively in the yard, knowing they couldn't afford her. He sold her to a man who arrived during a short break in the downpour. He sat confidently inside the Benz for a few minutes, then paid in cash from a bulky briefcase. Robert noticed he had a gold tooth that glinted in the watery sunlight each time he smiled. The Benz seemed a little sullen as she drove away, but Robert told himself he'd made a tidy profit and felt no regret.

Preparing for bed that night, as the rain beat against the shutters of their bedroom window, Robert asked if he could brush his wife's hair. She didn't seem to notice that his hands were shaking, nor did she ask him why he crawled into her embrace as soon as she turned off the bedside lamp. She just smiled, held him and drifted peacefully off to sleep.

Soothed by her soft breathing, Robert eventually slept. He dreamt he was being pursued through the narrow back streets of his childhood and woke with his heart pounding. He lay in his wife's arms, listening to the persistent patter of the rain, until the first light of day slid through the dripping shutters.

He saw the Benz again about three months later, on one of those clear, cool December days just after the end of the rainy season. Glancing in his rearview mirror as he balanced his mobile phone on his shoulder, Robert felt a jolt so strong the receiver fell unheeded into the passenger seat. Her chrome gleamed in the midday sun, as she crouched, purring in the line of cars. No other car on the road could hold a candle to her.

Almost against his will, Robert let the Benz pass him and then followed her through the city traffic, honking at pedestrians and nearly knocking an old man off his moped in his anxiety. He saw naked admiration in the eyes of four men who were playing a game of dominoes at a roadside rum bar as she drove by them. Then she left the busy city streets and headed towards the avenues of peaceful, prosperous houses. They had driven together here when she'd first come into his life, he realised. With the rains, the bougainvillea had sprouted long, thorny shoots. The hibiscus leaves were tight, green and glossy, pushing into the road. A gardener, struggling to cut them back, stopped and stepped into the shadow of the hedges to let the cars pass.

The Benz turned up into the foothills and onto a quiet, dirt road that ran along the side of a river valley. Soon Robert was driving between crumbling rock held in place by clumps of stubborn Guinea grass and a precipitous drop to a narrow stream that ran thirty feet below. He decided to stay a discreet distance behind her.

He thought he'd lost sight of her until her glittering chrome winked at him from a small side road. Heart thumping, Robert drove carefully down the steep, narrow track towards the river. The bush grew so thickly on both sides he could see nowhere but straight ahead. The track ended in a sunny clearing at the river's edge.

The Benz was not alone. She'd come here, made him follow her here, to meet someone. On a small sandy beach twenty yards from where he stopped, there were scattered clothes, a picnic hamper, a crumpled blanket. Over the soft roar of the water, Robert heard the laughter of a man, and a woman. Parked beside the Benz, almost hidden in the shade of a clump of feathery bamboo, was a familiar estate car.

Sadness washed over Robert in deepening waves. He took a last, lingering look at the Benz. Set against the rich greenery of the riverbank, her chrome seemed to dance in the sunlight. Humiliated, Robert reversed quietly into the shadow of the track. It had, after all, been true love.

The Great White Hate
Courttia Newland

There was a noticeable bounce in his step, a bounce that had turned his normal loose-limbed stride into a confident strut of serenity. With head held high, arms swinging confidently by his sides and eyes that scanned the surroundings with the enquiring gaze of a newborn, Marcus felt on top. Everything seemed fresh, exciting, alive with colours he'd taken for granted the previous day. Before she'd let him know. He could literally feel the blood rushing through his veins. He wanted to make his joy known to the entire world as last night, he'd finally convinced June to stop taking the Pill, so they could try for the child he'd wanted for so long.

   She hadn't been too hot on the idea at first. She was a beautiful girl, Asian-English, and lively, sexy, down to earth, independent – everything Marcus loved in a woman. But as a struggling actress she'd always believed kids would hinder her career. And she couldn't allow anything to get in her way. But

Marcus had pleaded and complained and begged and badgered, even offering to become a househusband, if she'd just take nine months out...

She'd laughed when he said he'd have the baby for them, if he could. That was when she'd relented, and finally agreed.

Strolling through the Kipling Estate, sipping a lemon Oasis, he was on top of the world until a cry from a fast moving car reached his ears. He looked up, open-mouthed, as it shimmied and stopped a block away. The blood-blotched face of a local Jack the Lad leaned out of the window and repeated the words Marcus thought he'd imagined.

'Fackin' Nigga!' came the cry, before the young man followed up with an additional salvo. 'Go back home ya fackin' coon! Ya not fackin' wanned 'ere!' Then the car screeched off the sound of tyres wailing and echoing around the block.

Marcus felt his good cheer flow out of him with the speed of blood pumping through a major artery. He gripped the Oasis bottle tight in his hand, then started to run, his long legs pumping and his eyes full of rage. At first the driver didn't see him. They'd expected him to stand and watch, so although they took off with a lot of noise, they'd been more or less cruising their way down the block, secure in the thought that, to them, he was just another spineless wog.

But Marcus was a hell of a lot more than that. He'd almost caught up with the vehicle, before the same blotchy-faced man in the passenger seat saw him and alerted the driver. The car lurched forward, then picked up speed. There was an intersection at the bottom of the road and Marcus was sure he'd never catch them. Hi-octane rage fuelled his headlong run, but, although his attempt was valiant, he knew he wasn't going to make it. A roar of anger rose in his throat, as the vehicle took a sudden right turn. He threw his half-filled bottle at the car.

Everything happened in an instant. He saw the bottle smash

against the window, and the driver's look of panic as lemon juice flew over the window. He saw him twist the wheel, too late to avoid the missile. Then the car disappeared from view.

Immediately afterwards Marcus heard a screech of tyres, then the sounds of crunching metal and shattering glass.

A deadly silence fell.

He stopped running, his brain taking over his defensive instinct, the fear flooding his body…

Shit. They crashed, he told himself, forcing his brain to believe it. I made them crash…

Around the corner the sight was worse than he could've imagined. From the tyre marks on the road, Marcus could clearly see what had happened. The car had swerved left, bounced into some parked cars, then careened across the road until it hit a metal railing. It then dragged the railing a few yards, before hitting a black Victorian-style lamppost, and coming to a violent stop. When he saw the broken glass and the wreckage of the steaming car, the young man fought an urge to run, run as fast as he possibly could. No one would believe him if he told them what'd happened – it'd be a clear case of white vs black. He'd be better off escaping and leaving their lives in the hands of fate.

But when he turned to go, he found his legs forcing him the opposite way – moving towards the wreckage, stepping unwillingly closer. Like it or not, he'd played a part in this scene, there was no way he could deny it. He steeled himself as he got closer still.

There were people coming out of nearby terraced houses to see what all the noise was about; he waved them back with a shaking hand and told them to stay away. His first sight as he peered through the windows, was the blood… He could see it already and it instantly made him feel queasy. There were four people in the car – Marcus hadn't seen the two in the back and was shocked to see a young girl, who looked no older than sixteen. Her face was covered in a red mess, and her head was thrown back, her mouth open wide.

Marcus retched painfully, then reached for the passenger door and found it locked. Without thinking, he pushed his arm through the shattered glass, snaking his hand downwards and pulling at the lock. Quick as he could, he pulled his arm back.

'Shit!'

Pain, as intense and insistent as a paper cut of grand scale. Marcus looked at his hand. Glass from one of the windows had torn a chunk of flesh away, leaving a bloody gash. The full pain, and the blood, hadn't reached it yet. He looked at his injury, cursing his bad luck.

'Don't move them!' Marcus heard from behind him. Forgetting his cut hand, he turned to see a middle-aged man standing on the pavement, watching. Marcus pointed at the cars crumpled bonnet.

'I gotta move 'em, that engine'll be fucked, an' it might even blow...'

'I think you've been watching too many movies, young man.'

Marcus gave him a hard glare, then sighed and looked around at the silent crowd. 'Has anyone phoned an ambulance yet?'

Bingo. There was a multitude of shocked and embarrassed faces.

'I'll go.' A fat greying lady, boasting wobbly triple chins, moved with surprising speed into her house. Marcus turned back to the car and, together with a young white guy, eased the injured youths from the car. The pain in his palm now yelped for attention, but he paid it no mind – even though the weight of the car's passengers made him want to scream in agony. The man in the passenger seat was unconscious, a large purple bump already growing on his forehead. His hair glistened with blood as though he'd been bathing in it. The driver however, was conscious, and although he allowed himself to be pulled from the car, when he was on the pavement, he opened his eyes and glared hatefully at Marcus.

'Git your 'ands off me ya black bastard,' he muttered, through clenched, yellowed teeth. Marcus looked up to see if anyone had heard and saw his young helper, looking straight into his eyes in shock.

Good, he thought, at least he heard.

He stepped away from the men and waited for the ambulance.

Sirens and engines roaring towards him. Arguments with one of the paramedics followed, who didn't want to let him ride with the injured. Marcus, insisting he had to come... Casualty, and that all-too-familiar waiting, on those all-too-familiar hard plastic chairs. Waiting, waiting, waiting...

Marcus blinked and looked at his watch, then his clothes. An hour had passed since the accident, and he'd been in the waiting room for an eternity. June would be missing him by now – he knew this, and felt bad, but he had to see it through, had to see the end result. To be truthful, progress was slow – hardly anyone had moved in all the time he'd been there. A black guy with a makeshift bandage around his head had been there long before Marcus, and still hadn't been seen, even though he'd complained. Good old NHS, he thought to himself derisively. The only way to get quick service here was to be on death's door.

He put his head in hands, then felt the stickiness and took them away. His hands, his shirt and his jacket had large patches of blood all over them. He should've washed, but his legs felt weak, and he didn't trust them to carry him. Guilt was thriving in his mind like a poisonous mushroom – attractive, yet deadly if consumed. His mind kept replaying the moment he'd thrown the bottle, wishing he could go back and change what he'd done...

Swing doors squeaked open. He looked up to see a couple he

recognised from the estate. The man was in his forties, short and full of wrinkles with a musty-looking cap on his balding head. His wife was large, with deep-set eyes, long brown hair and no shape to her middle-aged body. They spoke to the receptionist, and Marcus heard the man mention the boys in the road accident, before he and his wife sat down.

Marcus found his guilt forcing him up, making him cross the space between him and them, making him stare down into their grief-filled faces.

'Excuse me…'

They looked up as one, puzzled, then annoyed.

'Piss off will ya? We ain't got no money.'

They looked at him closer, noticing the blood on his clothes.

'Sorry to disturb you… I jus' wanted to know if it's your son who was involved in the car crash?'

'What business is it–' the man started.

The woman elbowed his side, then looked up at Marcus.

'It was our sons. What's it gotta do wiv you?'

Marcus felt his heart rate climbing. 'Well, I have to confess…'

'Confess?'

That was the mother.

'…It was my fault your sons crashed… in a way… See, they were screaming racist abuse at me…'

'Your fault!' The father was up in an instant, pushing a leathery face in his, breath stinking of stale cigarettes. Marcus backed away and attempted to overpower the man with his voice. The receptionist and the other people waiting looked around worriedly.

'So I chased 'em and threw a bottle at 'em, that made 'em crash… I didn't mean fuh that to happen, it jus' did… I'm sorry about yuh son…'

'*Sons* you little fackin' cunt! You black bastard, dere woz two brothers in dere! Hol' me back, Maud, or I'll kill 'im, I swear I will!' He lunged for Marcus, but the younger man easily wrestled himself loose and ran towards the exit.

The doctor arrived.

'Go back to the jungle ya coon!' said the man, edging in a last word as he turned towards the doctor. 'They come over 'ere, get fed an' looked after, then they start killin' innocent white kids... Go back to Africa!'

Outside the hospital, he slowed down, taking much-needed deep breaths. It was a long time since he'd had to listen to that kind of shit, and it brought him back to the real world with a bang. English people were normally smart with their racism. Choosing not to shout or scream that you weren't wanted, simply moving away from you as if you were a leper when you came down the street.

He needed June. He needed to forget about today's incident and start thinking about his future son or daughter. He needed to make love to his woman.

Marcus headed home.

At the hospital the accident victims' father looked towards the exit in disgust. 'Ee's done a runner, black cunt!'

The doctor asked the receptionist who Marcus had been. She told him the youth had apparently rescued the accident victims. The doctor asked if he'd left a name or address where he could be contacted. She shook her head.

'Ee put 'em there! Ee killed my sons!' The doctor gave the man a strange look.

'Your sons are far from dead, Mr Fisk. Now if you'd like to follow me...'

They walked down a busy corridor, the doctor showing them into a small room, with comfortable chairs, flowers and simplistic pictures covering the walls. They sat down, looking nervous and tense. The doctor closed the door behind him. The large woman looked up at him, her eyes full of tears.

'You said they're far from dead, Doctor, but they're dyin' aint they? I've seen Casualty, I know what dis room means…'

'Shut up woman,' her husband spat.

The Doctor ignored them. He was a gaunt, clinical-looking man, and surveyed them from behind thick spectacles that made his blue eyes glow and swim like tropical fish. 'Mr Fisk, Mrs Fisk. Like I said before, your sons are far from dead. Their passengers are far from dead.'

'I didn't know there were passengers,' Mr Fisk muttered, puzzled.

'In fact, all they're suffering from is slight concussion and superficial cuts and bruises. But, see, the thing is, we need to talk seriously with anyone that's been in physical contact with Aiden since the crash, especially the black youth…'

The Fisks fell silent.

'I'm sorry to have to tell you this, but during our efforts to transfuse blood into Aiden, we found strong indications that he's HIV positive.'

And meanwhile, elsewhere, Marcus walked home – his cut hand throbbing painfully – trying to forget the last few hours, wanting to wrap his arms around his woman and give her something they could both share…

Joy
Patsy Antoine

Oba ko so...

The words come to me strong, loud, louder... hard syllables juxtaposed in unfamiliar couplings. I sense a wrench, a coming apart and a pulling upwards. I open my eyes and I'm floating, all around me a dense grey fog.

He'd always said it was here.

I see his face as it was that last time. 'I won't leave you, Jus,' he'd said. He'd smiled at me then, the way he always did. A wide grin parting his brown lips. Lips that'd never failed to turn me on, but were now often hiding a pain I couldn't feel. Burnished brown skin belying the pallor of an illness out of control...

Minute droplets of water dampen my skin. My skin? I look down at my hands, ghost-like in the thickening mist. Brown skin turned bronze, translucent almost in the haze. I make a circle with my hand and it creates individual snapshots of movement that fade in seconds, my own ghostly reminder that this place is beyond time.

I wish myself forward and my body responds, gliding forwards as if propelled by some silent engine. My mother always said a wish is power. I never understood what she meant. Until now...

We'd both seen the babalawo on the same day. A hot day in August whilst holidaying in Atlanta. Our hosts had both had destiny readings done and we'd shared their enthusiasm for readings of our own. Marcus had been interested, though never indulged, in ifa for some time. His mother, a Nigerian and deeply spiritual, practised the religion and had been encouraging him to become involved since she'd first been initiated a couple of years before.

'I just want to know my purpose for being here,' he'd said.

I'd nodded, smiled, agreed.

Making the appointment had been easy.

The babalawo was a serene and humble man whose age was difficult to fathom. His front room was a shrine to ifa with an altar of rum, rosy apples, chilli peppers and red candles built into an alcove by the window. The late afternoon sun filtered through a muslin net across the window and candles burned all around the room.

I felt calm in his presence as he slowly, meticulously divined my purpose. 'It is to find joy,' he said. 'It may seem simple, but yours is a complex reading.' It didn't make sense to me at the time. I'd already found that joy in Marcus. He was the other half in my divine making. My mate. My soul. My king. His queen. I lived a happy life, what more joy could I want? Or need? I thanked him and left the room, waiting for Marcus in the small hallway. I'd spent over an hour with the priest and so I settled myself in for a long wait, but just fifteen minutes later the door opened and Marcus emerged.

'I'm here to teach,' he said, disappointed. He was already a secondary school teacher and had been hoping for a more esoteric reading like mine.

'What else did he say?' I'd asked.

'Nothing,' he mumbled, much too quickly.

Oba ko so…

The words come again. Persistent, desperate, calling me forwards. A ball of urgency snowballs in my stomach and I visualise speed. Before me a humming bird materialises, suspended in the air, in effortless glory. Green and gold and ochre in hue, a blur of wings holding her motionless. Movement too fast to see.

Then I, too, have wings. I sense the weight of their power, their strength. The speed I now have propels me forward, air rushing to meet me as I slice my way through the fog.

I think of my earthly body and a hint of terran grief threatens to invade my calm. As I speed through this time and space I'm wondering what I'll find. I sense laughter, tears. Extremes of emotion…

We'd made love that Saturday morning. The best kind. The kind of sex you have in the haze of dawn, the memory of which lasts the entire day. Our passion had brought tears to my eyes and afterwards we'd dozed then woken and gone again. But in our post-coital serenity there was a sadness in Marcus's spirit that he'd denied when I pressed him.

It wasn't until later that he told me. He'd had tests, he said. Nothing to worry about. Just a small lump.

I feel myself slowing, great wings now visible as their humming eases. And as I stare hard into the mist it begins to dissipate. Patches of a jigsaw picture now becoming visible. Green. I feel, no, see, green. I'm still floating but now I'm hovering above the realness, the firmness of soil. The path I try to connect with is one of russet red, life-giving soil that's nutrient-rich and packed hard and firm. As I rest my foot down I feel nothing. Walking is not for me here.

Ahead of me I see a trellis archway and beyond it what looks like a rose garden. I'm drawn to this place and float effortlessly towards it. It feels comfortable, warm, familiar. This is my garden and within the confines of its rose bush boundaries I become solid once more...

Tests, chemo drugs, remission.
Tests, chemo drugs, remission.
Tests, chemo drugs, remission.
Tests, chemo drugs...
I'm lost. Confused. Devastated. How can I live on? My joy is gone...

Inside the rose garden one whole side has died. Flower heads withered and dried, the soil cracked and hard. I feel sad to see it. Sad that it has become so barren. The pain of loss is so acute here that I gasp and turn away.

I'm faced with an entirely different scene now. The garden here is lush and blooming with roses of fuschia, burnt orange and buttercup yellow. Butterflies quietly hover, bees pollinate and the smell of roses is pungent and earthy. Everything is alive, thriving, living...

Oba ko so...

Now the words seem calm, welcoming. I close my eyes and a third opens.

Enlightenment.

Foreign words, words from an ifa prayer, that are suddenly no longer foreign: Oba ko so. The king did not hang.

'Justine.'

I hear his voice in my mind and when I open my eyes he's there, standing among the lush rose bushes, my humming bird hovering near his shoulder. He looks healthy, glowing in what looks like cream linen. Not as he was in the last days, but as I remember him in our early times together. He is ghost-like and hovers above the ground, but his spirit is strong, grounded somehow. He's here in this place, my place, truly here and he smiles.

And I finally know where to truly find joy.

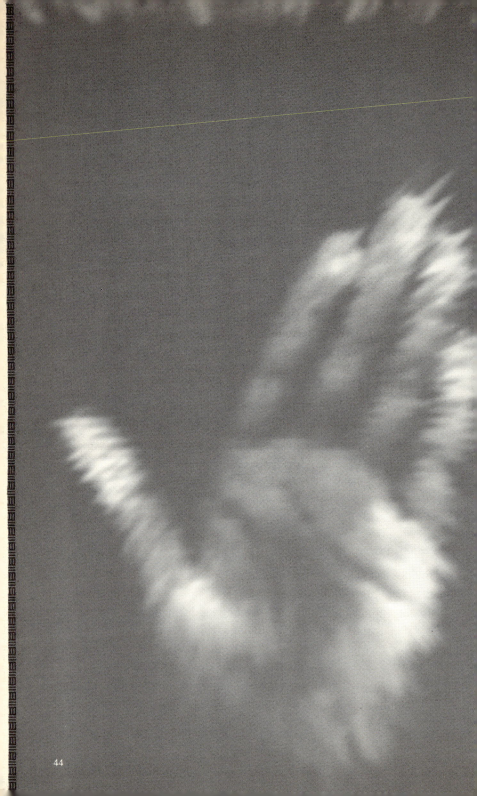

Johnny Can Sleep Easy Now
JJ Amaworo-Wilson

Sometimes I look at Johnny and it makes me want to weep. He's like a bird with a broken wing. Nothing can pull him back into the air where he once was.

We cut the corner of Acklam Road, past the iron skeletons of market stalls and emerge from under the bridge into the face of a hard, driving rain. The lights are going down in bedsit land and the creepy crawlies are coming out of their holes: dealers, pushers, pimps, prostitutes, assuming their positions for the pantomime of night. A car glides by, smooth as glass, catching the lights in its windows; slows down and accelerates again across the hush of London.

I was born in a hot country not so long ago.

Johnny came back with a flower tattooed on his arse and a million bruises that weren't there before. He doesn't say anything, but prison's in his eyes. Four walls and four hundred National

Front cunts with the habits of rottweilers. No wonder he sleeps with a knife in his hand.

We're past Westbourne and the rain's building into something bigger, amassing itself at the edge of the road. It lashes us, but we keep moving till Barney says, 'Wait a minute. I need some smokes.' And I hear the ring of the door that he pushes open. The sawn-off Paki's trembling in his nylons because Barney's known around here, but he turns and plucks out twenty Marlboro Reds and does the transaction and we're walking again.

'Fuckin' Pakis,' Barney says. But I'm dealing with the rain.

Johnny's horizontal. He doesn't stand much since they ripped up his tendons with a Stanley knife. We parked him on a mound of cushions in the fleapit and Barney brought a telly so the hours would pass. He smokes like fuck, rolls them one-handed, even with the shakes, and Barney doesn't like it but what can you do.

We're over on Talbot and getting closer when Barney pauses under the neck of the streetlamp and I see the flicker of the flame in his hand, and the phantom of smoke rise and dissipate from his mouth. The sky is a no-colour. If you put grey, blue and orange in the mixer, this is what you'd get. It's the colour of a dying animal, something going rotten in the city's neon machine.

I remember when I was a boy and mum took us home, me, Barney and Johnny. And the sky went on forever and all you could see was blue. I must have been five, maybe six. The sea and the sky and sand in between my toes. Our mother laughing and Johnny unbruised.

I'm nearly lost now. I don't know these streets the way Barney does. They say a rat always knows the way to food, and I guess Barney always knows the way to trouble. We pass tower blocks and shadows and cubes of glass and stone, like giant pieces of Lego left in the rain. Everything is grey and everything is caught in reflections off the patches of water under our feet.

A collapsed bin empties itself into our slice of pavement, white papers and cartons and the glint of polythene, and it looks like an open mouth vomiting trash.

When I think of Johnny I don't think of him the way he is now. I see his long legs taking the escalator steps three at a time, with me following. He is the firstborn so I will always be following him in my head. But not in my body, not now. He's the blackest of us. Then Barney. Then me. It's like we were getting more and more diluted.

He did some bad things and they put him away. The judge fucked him up, that's what Barney says. First offence. No damage to nobody. A housebreak through a window he didn't even kick the door down. And the judge gave him two years because he's a brother.

We turn a corner and suddenly we're there. Barney kicks at the door and the latch comes away in an explosion of splinters. One more kick with the flat of his boot and it springs open with a shower of dust like confetti, and we're in. We're running now, down an unlit corridor, till we reach the end. Barney turns left so I catch his profile in the darkness. He steps back. Another kick. The door flies off its hinges and he walks in. I follow. There's a scramble and some guy, a black guy, short dreads, red dishonest eyes, half-naked is trying to get out of a window. Barney pulls him back in and rams him against a wall.

'I ain't done nuffink!' The man screams it but Barney's already punching his face hard so his head keeps smacking against the wall. Barney hits him four times till the guy's sliding down the brickwork.

'Johnny Walcott. D'you remember Johnny Walcott?' The guy doesn't move or speak.

'Johnny Walcott. You did a job with him two years ago. You sold him out. He did time. Do you remember?' The guy still doesn't speak. I hear voices along the corridor. Suddenly Barney's pulled a knife and he moves it left to right in one fluid swing and there's a spray of blood. The guy starts gurgling and Barney's off him.

'Let's go,' he says and drags me. But I'm transfixed. This guy on the floor is spouting blood from his neck and his hips are shuddering, but Barney just pulls my arm. 'Let's get the fuck out of here.'

We run past two figures in the dark of that corridor and keep running for maybe six minutes, till we hear the howl of sirens. We're in shadow. Barney hauls me up against a fence and slaps me the way I've seen him slap Maddy, his girl.

'Next time I say go, you go.'

Then he plugs my face with a Marlboro Red and cuffs me lightly, laughing. 'Johnny can sleep easy now,' he says.

It pours down long into the night. There is no break. No ceasing of the momentum. I lie awake and listen to a gunshot of lightning break out of the slow and steady hiss of the rain. Across the roofs of London, water is congregating. Its diagonals are caught like metal needles in the headlights of cars moving from night into morning.

I am fifteen years old and the rain won't stop.

49

The Car
Lucas Loblack

I can see my death coming. A wall rushing at me. Impact. Screeching metal. I jerk backwards, forwards. My head smacks the steering wheel. Silence. No thought. I can feel nothing, see only smoke. Voices whisper at me, insistent, asking me to stand up. I do just that. I want to see who's talking to me, who seems to be leaning over my shoulder. But then I find myself outside the car, gazing at the mutilated bonnet. My body's inside, bloodied and bent over the dashboard. I sway, suddenly feeling very stoned...

Andrea?
Yes, Mummy?
Come on! We're going to be late!
I'm coming, I'm coming. Where's Dad?
He's in the car. Are you ready?

Er, not really.
Come on, you'll be fine. It's your first day at school, not prison.
Yeah, sure...

Andrea, hi, it's Michael – remember? We met at Guy's wedding last week. Just thought I'd give you a call to see if you're free sometime soon. Maybe we could go to that vodka bar you were talking about... I'm sure I gave you my number, but just in case it's 0171 225...

Jesus, Andrea! Slow down!
Sorry, Sarah, I can't find my bloody watch.
It's on the table next to the sofa.
Thanks... Oh shit! My fucking tights are torn!
I'm making some coffee. Do you want one?
Er, sure. I just have to get changed...
I thought you said the meeting started at ten?
It does, but I have to go over some figures with Adam first. I'm supposed to be there in half an hour.
Are you still off sugar?
Yeah, but listen Sarah, I don't think I'll have time to finish it. God, I'm so late!
Your mobile's on the windowsill, if that's what you're looking for.
Sarah, you're a star. Look, I've got to go. Sorry about the coffee.
Don't worry about it. Are you back this evening?
Yes... er, no. I'm meeting Michael for dinner, probably stay at his place...

It's the Bam Bam Breakfast, Kiss 100... Busta Rhymes with Gimme Some More... Freedom at Bagleys, Saturday night... But first the travel...

You stupid slag! Need your eyes testing do ya? Red means stop!

Fuck off you moron!

Thursday? Sorry can't do that, I've got a meeting then lunch with the guys from The Guardian. No, it's another big promo. I've got to do a presentation for our flagship titles coming out over Christmas. Yeah right, you and the rest of the world. As soon as copies come in you'll get one. No, that one comes out in April, in hardback. I'm busy in the evening as well. How about Friday? Damn. Okay, look, how about next Tuesday? I'm free all afternoon so maybe we can make a session of it? Great. And let's try somewhere else this time, I'm getting bored of the same old pasta... And don't give me that "Oh Andrea, dahhrling," crap either. Oh sure, like I've really got an expense account that big. It's your shout this time, especially if we're going there. Great! Pick me up at eight. No, outside the office, it's easier to park. Late, me?

Andrea? It's Dave. Call me please. It's about Mum...

Listen, Andrea, maybe you should call the police.
That's what Sarah said. She reckons I can get him for stalking.
Well he is stalking you, isn't he?
He's always hanging around, but he doesn't do anything.
Yeah, right, if you call chucking acid all over your car not doing anything. What if he decides to throw acid over you?
Oh come on, Jackie, don't start freaking me out.
I mean it, Andrea. He's the freak, not you. Do something about it, please.

The VW?
Yeah, pump number seven. And 20 Silk Cut Ultra as well please.
Have you got an Express Points card?
No.

Up to 25 per cent off with your first 50 points –
Look, sorry, I'm in a hurry...

Pure spirit, pure Smirnoff. Kiss 100. Traffic and weather coming up...

Dad?
Hmmm?
Is it true what Dave said?
About what?
About you and Mum getting me a car if I get a 2:1.
Maybe.
Oh come on, dad. It's true, isn't it?
You'll find out when it happens...

jasonkay@hotmail.com. Wow! I don't believe it! Zanzibar. It sounds like a dream. Bloody hell, Jason, how come you never mentioned that part of your journey? It's the usual stuff back here – still hate my job, still haven't found a place to buy yet and Ray's still hanging around. And you were right, by the way, he is a git...

Adam! Why didn't you let me know sooner? I'm nearly there now!
Sorry Andrea, I meant to but I got caught up. Jimmy started vomiting again and –
Okay, okay. Don't worry about it. I suppose there isn't that much to go over. What time do you think you'll make it in?
Maybe 9-9.30. I just tweaked the backlist figures here and there, but you can have a look at what I've done. I left the documents with Hannah. She said she'd be in early.
Okay, thanks. What about Stephen's report?
Hannah's got that too. She ran off a couple of copies last night. I, er... well, I briefed her just in case.

Oh great. It would've been nice if you'd briefed me, too.
Andrea, sorry, I –
Can't talk now, lights have changed. See you later...

Fatboy Slim in happy, hippie mode. Just before 8 am... You're listening to Kiss 100...

Blimey, Andrea! You've kept that one quiet. He sounds wonderful... Yeah, well, it's about time you got lucky... Yeah, I know, Sarah mentioned it. You really ought to do something about it, Andrea. But that's not the point. He's harassing you just by being there!... Hmmm. I still think you should lodge a complaint or something... Just concentrate on Michael. He sounds like a dish. So, when do I get the chance to meet him?...

Andrea. It's Dave. Are you still coming over on Saturday?... I could do with some moral support. I'm bringing Stacey to meet everyone, and you know what mum's like, she'll cook for bloody Christmas...

The millennium? I don't know. I haven't really thought about it. Why?
Well... Andrea, how about coming to Kenya with me?
Kenya? Michael, are you serious?
Yes. I've, er... I've booked the tickets.
To Kenya? When?
Last week. I wanted to tell you on Thursday but things were a bit rushed.
Bloody hell... Kenya... For how long?
Three weeks, if you can get the time off.
Believe me, honey, I'll get the time off!
So, does that mean yes?
God Michael! Of course it does! I'll start packing!

Heavy traffic at the Hogarth Roundabout... Kiss 100 exclusive...

Piss off!
Sunday driver!

Mum, Dad, I'll never forget this – thank you.
And don't go mad. I know what you're like.
Oh come on, Dad. I know what I'm doing, I'm not like the other nutters on the road.
Darling, haven't you forgotten something...
Er... Thanks mum. Can't get very far without the keys, can I?
Be careful!
I will, I promise!...
jasonkay@hotmail.com... Guess what? I'm going to Kenya!

Kiss 100 in the mix... Happening at the The End on Friday night... Listen out for that on the Rap Chart, Wednesday night... Traffic coming next...

Hi Hannah... Yes, fine thanks... I know, he called... Look, I'll be there in 10 minutes or so. Would you get that stuff sorted out for me please?... Is he? Bloody hell! What for?... What?! And their MD as well?... Oh God... No, don't bother, I'll leave a note for Katie... Er, listen, I'd better sign off. I need to think... No, I'm fine, honestly. See you in a mo...

Bloody hell, Jackie! Stop hassling me. I'll do something about it, okay?!... Yes, yes! I'll report him... I will!... Promise...

When?... This Saturday? Hmmm... Sounds good but I can't say for certain. I was planning to stay at Michael's this weekend, I've hardly seen him all week. Did I tell you he's taking me to Kenya for the millennium?... Neither can I! He's booked the tickets and everything! And guess what? He gave me this really beautiful ring – sorry, hang on, Kate's waving something at me... Thanks... Oh for god's sake... No, don't worry, I'll deal with it. Thanks Kate... Sorry about that... No, just another bloody fax about shit... Sure. And I'll get back to you about the Stonehenge thing... Sounds good. I'll let you know... God, not you as well! What's the matter with everyone?... Yeah, yeah, you'll get your signed copy, don't worry... No, he didn't mention it. Why?... Sounds serious... Er, sure, but it'll have to be a quick one. I'm meeting Michael at eight... Yes, I know the one. They serve great vodka...

R&B night at Bar Rumba, and David Rodigan going extra large at Gossips... Kiss 100. One hundred per cent music... News and travel next...

Hi, Sarah... Yes, I know, he just called...
Something about his baby throwing up all over the place.
Yeah, he told me.
Well, I thought I'd call, just in case. Also... and er, you're not going to like this Andrea...
Try me.
You left your transparencies behind –
Oh for fuck's sake!
I spotted them on the way out...
God! I hate this fucking day already!
Is there anything I can do?
No... no. Thanks, Sarah. I'm almost at the office now – if only that fucking Land Rover would get out of the bloody way! What the hell are you doing? Arsehole!
Look, Andrea, I'd better go –
Yeah, right, sorry about that.
I'll leave your file by the door in case you decide to come back.

Great, thanks Sarah. See you later...

Andrea. It's Dave. Jackie told me what happened, you know, about Ray throwing acid over your car... Look, why don't you let me sort him out? I'll just talk to him, quietly, if you understand me – just me and a coupla friends...

andrea.henry@giganticpublishing.co.uk... Good luck for this morning. Hope you knock 'em dead! See you this evening – and don't be late! Love, M.

The Miseducation of Lauren Hill *and before that Jayzee with* Hard Knock Life... *Kiss 100 in the mix... But first the travel...*

Right means right, you sick bastard!... What the – ? Jesus! Shit!... Oh God, oh God, I can't brake! Jesus! I can't brake...

I can see my death coming. A wall rushing at me. Impact. Screeching metal. I jerk backwards, forwards. My head smacks the steering wheel. Silence. No thought. I can feel nothing, see only smoke. Voices whisper at me, insistent, asking me to stand up. I do just that. I want to see who's talking to me, who seems to be leaning over my shoulder. But then I find myself outside the car, gazing at the mutilated bonnet. My body's inside, bloodied and bent over the dashboard. There's someone sitting beside me – a shadow in the passenger seat. He looks like Michael but feels like Ray. Bright light everywhere. I sway, suddenly feeling very stoned...

Who Am I?
Natalie Stewart

I've been a leader
Bore a leader
Nursed a leader
Raised a leader
Counselled a leader
And loved a leader
All in one lifetime.
My lifetime.
A lifetime that's mine.

Checking my celestial lifeline
You'll see that's equivalent to a whole heap of time.
See, I am the person that my ancestors advised me to be.
The personality they chose
To control the destiny they began to form
And they are the reason that I am.
Their experience guides me away from those who
can't be trusted
And encourages me to trust myself
My better judgement is a collaboration of their thoughts
And my inspiration a fusion of their courage
Their anger gives fuel to my soul
And their blood decorates my words
As I speak the truth of my past, present and future
Adding strength to the battle
And encouraging the revolution.
So... who am I?
Your question should have been answered a thousand times
A thousand lifetimes and more.
I am the decision to stand
When the option was to fall.
I am the idea
The opinion
The suggestion
The thought
I am the enlightenment
As well as the darkness that surrounds it.
I am living proof
For the living who need proof
As their faith isn't strong enough
I am so hard to define
Jealousy created taboo language.
I am history

I am present
I am future
I am education
I am science
I am nature.
I am all of this
Yet to you I am a stranger.
But all of this I am.
Who are you?

The Price of Maybe
Kadija Sesay

I wonder how he's changed. His moustache was so tickly and sexy. I remember that's what made my waters run the first time we met. The neat way each hair lay above his morello lips. They begged me. I just had to kiss him. Deep lust, heavy like. I should have stuck to that formula, instead of falling in love. Marrying him and breeding so damn quickly. It all turned into such a mess. I didn't help matters much by running away. But it was the only way out I could see at the time. Rahim couldn't see that anything was wrong. He thought he was perfect for me. He thought we were perfect together! But I remember how he loved to point out my flaws. I hated him undermining me in front of the children. Hmm. I remember those times too often. Like when he would point at my legs and say I had crocodile skin, all dry and scaly, just to make them laugh. I never said anything. I just let him hug me, smother me, as I let all the embarrassment and frustration soak in. His love always masked it. He couldn't see the worms that squirmed around in me sometimes. Worms that turned into maggots and festered. At other times I felt just like a mouse. I would watch him, scared, as he unlocked his jaws, sucked and smothered and swallowed me whole. He was crazy. He loved to eat me whole. Although I must admit, sometimes it was nice. Looking back, it wasn't all bad, I suppose. I hope he's forgiven me. I'm sure he has. He must've done if he wants to see me. Divorce? Does he want a divorce? It hasn't been that long. I haven't even found my feet without him yet. I can't be dealing with that now, too. I should have asked him. Girl, ya stupid! You should have made an excuse and said that because you're applying for residency, you can't leave the country yet. But you probably would have beat up on yourself, wouldn't you? I'm too scared to think about it. Probably the reason I didn't ask. The children are okay, I know that. Do they know I love them and didn't leave because of them? Did he give them the presents I sent? Did he read my letters to them? I wonder what he's told them. Why the hell are you thinking about this now, you're just going to make it more complicated. Hell, it was always complicated, but it's a good time to talk to him about the kids. They can come and live with me soon… just as soon as I get my residency sorted out. It'll be good to see him again – but I'm so scared. Why should I be scared? This time away from him has made me stronger, not so easily sucked in by him like a vacuum cleaner – hasn't it? Plane's coming in to land. Trust it to be raining. It doesn't give me a good feeling.

She's going to take this bad. I know she is. Even though she was the one who left me. And the kids. Rashid looks just like me and Rashida is my little Ami who looks so much like her mother, bites the right corner of her bottom lip like her mother, snuffles and twitches her nose, like her mother – how could she leave so much of herself with me? So, what the hell do I care how she takes it. She has no choice really. She made her choice without any thought for me, how I would miss her, loved her. How much I would cry for her. Real fucking tears cry for her. I remember when Rashida saw me like that. She hugged me, her tiny nostrils lifted up like Ami's and that just made me cry even more. She has me wrapped around her little finger, they both do. I would've done anything for her, anything. Remember the time she asked me to pick up her friend from the airport: waited all day because the flight was late, and I didn't even blow a fuse when the friend turned out to be an ex-lover. She had so many damn male friends. At least she didn't ask him to stay – it would've been just like her, and knowing me I would've let him, if it'd made her happy. 'But I'm your African girl now,' she said, matter-of-factly. As though it were ingrained, like Amina 4 Rahim, carved on a tree.

She just didn't give a shit that she was destroying our family. The kids just think she's away on a long trip. 'Mummy always said she wanted to go home and live in Africa. And when she's built the house, just like she built our tree house, we can go and live with her.' I've never told them any different, perhaps because I was always praying she would come back and take me home, too. This was such a stupid decision to meet her. I should've just telephoned, sent a letter. I didn't have to see her. I hope she doesn't look the same. Please, don't let her look the same. Every day I've tried to remove the picture of her face from everything I touch. I hope she doesn't smell the same. She always smelt of Ambrosia cream rice, topped with coconut. I can see her spooning it in to her mouth, giggling. Shit. Coconut. Is that what's in Rashida's shampoo? I thought it was baby shampoo. I'll have to check it when I get home. Damn. My heart is beating as fast as this train – and it's not slowing down with it, either. It's not fair on the kids and it's not fair on me. I have to get her out of my system. I have to stop breathing her in.

There he is! Oh my God – he looks just the same! I wonder if he smells the same! If he's used that cucumber and kelp soap I used to buy him, and then my favourite aftershave – the way it mixes with his body scent – oh no, don't. I hope the sweat doesn't start trickling from my armpits, down to waist to my... tickling like his fingers. If it does, I know I'm in trouble. I remember this feeling, I remember it so well. The last time I felt like this was when I told him I was pregnant with Rashid. He just melted. Like ice cream on cherries. He made every inch of me tickle that night. I gasped so much I almost stopped breathing. But it was worth it, the look on his face, his lips just heated up and became warmer. Where did it all go so wrong? He does smell the same. And he still has that moustache, slightly thinner perhaps. I hope he can't see the steam coming out of my eyes. My fanny's itching. Don't touch his hands! I didn't mean to snatch mine back quite like that. Sorry. No, I'm not sorry. I know what his look and smell could do – still does to me. If he comes any closer, I'll eat his lips! Why couldn't he just let me be me. Maybe it was the studying, that's it. Maybe he felt he needed to control me more because he wasn't working. But it didn't bother me. I don't understand why he didn't realise that. I never made him feel less important, did I? I thought he would be angry – he was just about to go back and study full time. A baby then – it was going to be so difficult. But we managed, didn't we? Let's just sit down. Then our eyes will be level. At least the noise in this airport is covering my nervousness. Concentrate, Ami, concentrate. Concentrate on what he's saying. His voice. Listen to his voice, his words, not his body. His body odour's in his voice too. What has he done, eaten the stuff? I'm sorry I didn't mean to snigger. I knows this is serious but I'm so nervous, I'm so scared of my nearness to you. Am I scared by the thought of what you're going to say? I'm not really listening, can you tell that? I'm just eating your smell. Your voice sounds harder than I remember. But maybe that's just how you are with me.

She looks even better. I knew she would. She's cut her hair short. Yes, it suits her like that. It highlights her cheekbones. Hell, she's a beautiful woman. I bet she only cut it to spite me, she knows I like her hair long. I used to go on and on at her about it. Braids always made her look younger, prettier, softer. I remember saying to her that she looked beautiful with hair, androgynous without it. Hmmm. She used to say that at least I knew what I was getting with her. The same way I see her at night, is what I get in the morning. No runaway braids, or greasy patch left on the pillow from a curly perm, no fingers caught in false hair. It was like her mantra, as soon as I opened my mouth and mentioned hair. She was right, I suppose. But she was beautiful with braids. And now, dammit, she's just as gorgeous without. God, not now, please. I don't want her to be making my groin hot, itchy with sweat. I have to be cool and off-hand about this. I'm not ready to see her yet. Does my hair look all right? Trimmed my moustache. I've shaved it the way she likes. No I didn't did I? Do it for her? I don't need her to be affecting me like this. I have someone else. I have someone else now. Okay, I'm ready. She's seen me. She wants to smile. Why doesn't she smile? She hates me. It's because she hates me. It's because I never let the kids go to her. Why should I? God, how did we end up like this. But it was her fault, too. Good. If I keep that in mind, I can deal with this. It's her fault and I have someone else. This is going to be easy. At least I can smile. Her skin is so soft, I'm not even that close to her, yet I can tell her skin is soft. Being in Africa is good for her. Shall I touch her? And she's still wearing our wedding ring! Shit! What does she think she's playing at? I bet she did it on purpose. What was our song, African girl, you're my African girl, you're the nicest girl for me in the whole wide world... That's what she was when I first met her and now this woman, no longer mine. I want my African girl back. I found her, I want her, she's mine. How dare she grow without me, away from me. Stupid. She never was yours and you were so arrogant you couldn't even tell. She told you in so many ways, and you ignored it every time. There was a time when you could have captured her and held her close, yet she fluttered through your fingers. What's this poetic shit now! Damn you Ami! I won't look in her eyes as I'm talking to her. I'll just look over her head, and imagine I'm talking to someone I don't like. Don't hug her. Don't smell her hair, don't hold her close. It was her fault, too. I have someone else now. She'll get the message.

Someone else. Someone else! How can he have someone else? How can he want someone else! Where were my children when he was fucking around? Where did he leave them? Don't tell me he was taking her into my house. My house! It's still my house. My bedroom. It was my money that paid the mortgage when he was staying home, studying for three years, three frigging years! Maybe it started then, when I was out working my butt off. It was my money that bought the bed he is sleeping comfortably in – they are sleeping in. How dare she! Who the hell does she think she is? Who is she? Sitting at breakfast with my kids as if she is their mother, I bet. I'll show her, she isn't. She doesn't know that Rashida only eats Sugar Puffs before she goes to school and Rashid doesn't like his omelette wet and soggy. How can she? She's not their mother. What's she feeding them? Like hell, she is stuffing them with English stodge. Steak and kidney pie. Take-away fish and chips. How could he allow that to happen? I'll kill Rahim. He should be glad we met in an airport lounge and that there are so many people around. I've got to get out of here. Just his presence is suffocating me. I bet he's even gone back to his slave name, too. Totally English-y. He only changed it when I insisted that my children had African names, when I showed him how spiritually unconnected he was. I'll kill him! How dare she! How dare she, bitch. Who is she? I want to know. How can I find out? I'll call Grace, she'll know. She's always been a good friend. She'll know what to do. I want her out. I have to get her out!

It was worse than I imagined. I still want her – so bad. I can't remember ever having my heart thud in my ears and knock against my chest. Damn her. How does she do it? Why couldn't I stop it? There I am standing, staring at her, thinking that if I open my mouth I can swallow her up, so she'll never leave me again. But my tongue goes thick, it fills my mouth so I can hardly talk. She must know from my eyes that I'm still crazy about her. Why can't she just massage the backs of my hands with her thumbs the way she used to? That's the only message I need to know that she still loves me. But she doesn't even look at me! She never really looked into my face did she? Now when I think about it, no, she didn't. Guilt. She felt bloody guilty. Well so she fucking should. They all told me to forget her. Remember? Mum said that I never should have married her, that she'll just go back to her own kind. I remember thinking, how could my own mum be so spiteful. God, just the smell of the coconut shampoo in her hair when I first stood over her was enough for me for the rest of my life. But she had to destroy it, didn't she? And I still don't understand why. That's what's really bugging me. I took care of her didn't I? Maybe I didn't listen. But she couldn't have gone because of that. No, I deserve to be mad. She shouldn't have gone like that. She could've talked to me first, told me she was unhappy and then I could have put it right. Why do women have to make their statements in such extreme ways? Why can't I just tell her I want her back? That's what this meeting was really all about, wasn't it? I want her in my arms, my bed. I want the smell of her coconut hair again...

What the hell am I going to do? What can I do? I've got to get my kids back. She's white. I can't have them being indoctrinated. They really will be black British then. They're African and they need to be in Africa, with me. He might not want to believe that he is, but my kids are. That should've told me we were wrong for each other. He never even saw himself as Bajan, just because he wasn't actually born there, but British. Yuk! My poor babies. I knew I should've taken them when I left. Getting them back is going to be so difficult now. But he always knew I'd come back for them. It isn't as if this arrangement is permanent. I never said I was going away forever. I just needed to breathe. What's the use in kidding myself about it now, though. Don't beat up on yourself, Amina, you barely got yourself out, let alone take the babies. You left because you had to. He was suffocating you, remember, chomping like a pacman on those old computer games. Rendering me unconscious. I was like a zombie. He has that strange sensual power over women, I've seen it. That's how he caught me. There were so many women in the room, but if he'd known I was African from the beginning, would he have been so greedy? I was taken in like every other woman. As soon as I saw him, I had to have him. It must have freaked him out as much as it did me. I should count myself lucky really. A light switched on in my head and I escaped in the end. Now let him zombify someone else!

I've just been using Helen as a way to block Ami out of my mind, my eyes, my life. But now that I've seen her again, what a mistake. It's like the past two years never happened! What a fool I've been, and she probably thinks I am, too. I bet she knew all along that I wanted to see her again. She must know I still love her. I even changed my name for her. I didn't hide it very well, did I? I don't think my stand-offish attitude was cold enough, but it's almost like I didn't want it to be. It's my own damn fault. That woman has turned me into such a mixed up motherfucker. I was warned about women like her, but I never thought Ami was one of them. I bet she's laughing at me this very minute. Thank God for Helen. My friends were right. White women don't turn the screw quite so tight the way our own women do. But she doesn't make me feel like Ami does. She doesn't satisfy my spirit in the same way. I want her back. I want Ami back. And Helen's been so supportive. Even when all I can do is sit down and mope around the house, thinking about Ami. She's put up with a lot from me. And she's still there! And she ain't laughing at me. She's my woman and I know where she is at because she's always there, waiting. Ami didn't wait for me. She ran off without me! Maybe that's why I find it so hard to forgive her.

But I'll keep the shampoo, maybe.

White Walls
Deborah Ricketts

I want to know something, feel something
For a reason, instead of being in here.
Here.
Being.
Two non-entities neither connecting nor creating a union.
Four walls, huge white walls,
Oh, they're draining me.
Not interested in what I'm paid to do
Need to change, or they will change me.
Locked up, caged up, strung up or strung out
It's no longer sustainable.
Nowhere to move to
Only to move out.
Move out to a new world
That's challenging and ever-changing
Always guided by the need to grow past this time and events.
Move on
      Move on
            Move on.

Trust Me
Brenda Emmanus

Dusk stole the last of the day, and slowed down the hubbub on Carling Road. Market traders wearily pushed stalls to secured lock ups and old men with rusty brown dentures seeped out of betting shops and made their way home along littered streets. The air was still warm from the surprisingly generous April sun, encouraging Claudia to take a slow stroll home from the station after a non-eventful day at work.

Outside her house four young men were gathered around the raised bonnet of a Suzuki Vitara. Discreetly, while retrieving her keys from a nylon rucksack, Claudia watched as one man craned his neck to look inside.

'Move out the way, man, you don't even know what you're looking for,' said a second younger man pushing roughly against the first.

'You can shut up, you don't even drive!'

As a chorus of laughter burst through the early evening air, Claudia chuckled to herself and walked the path to her front door. She hadn't laughed for a couple of days, it felt alien but pleasant.

Entering her house, she went into automatic pilot, flinging off her kitten-heeled mules, and throwing her keys into the straw basket on the corridor table. She slid pedicured feet into fake animal-print slippers and looked apprehensively at the answer machine.

Two messages.

Bet he hasn't called she thought. There was only one way to find out. As she watched the cassette rewind, Claudia felt a tightness in her throat and cramps in her stomach. She swallowed, then listened.

'Hi Claud, it's me, Leah. Hope you're well. Listen, I know he's getting to you, but don't worry. If you want a girlie night out just call me and we can go and get pissed. I could do with it, work's a bummer. Anyway, call me at home or on the mobbie. If I'm not around leave a message. Love you, bye!' She smiled for the second time that day, at least her best friend could be relied upon. She listened to the second message.

'Hi babes, w'happen?' It was Russell. 'Sorry, I've not been in touch these coupla days, but I've had a whole heap a tings to deal with, y'know. Anyway, maybe we can hook up next week. Carlton's deejaying at a party so I'm checking the boys tonight, and tomorrow I'm just gonna chill out. Speak to you soon, yeah.'

Claudia chewed on her bottom lip as she often did when angry. Why can't he see me tonight? Why can't I chill with him tomorrow? The bastard's up to something. He's at it again. She pushed the door and marched into her bedroom.

The green wooden door opened to reveal a flood of thick purple carpet. Complementary lavender walls flushed upwards kissing a high dado rail before transforming into fuschia pink.

The high carved ceiling revealed the age of the property. Late Victorian. Pine wardrobes lined one wall, bursting with compartmentalised seasonal garments, and a pine table below two wooden bookshelves boasted church candles, an incense burner and a framed Martin Luther King inspirational quote.

Claudia pulled a Lemongrass incense stick from a straw basket under the table, lit it, and stuck its bottom in the wooden incense burner. She turned on the portable TV but remained oblivious to its output. Life with Russell had become a yo-yo experience – from bliss to frustration, and back. When she was with him, they shared hours filled with youthful energy and explosive sexual chemistry. He'd managed to make her feel more relaxed and experimental with her body than any past lover, and his infantile spirit was a constant reminder of how pleasant life could be if kept simple. On the other hand, his absence caused her more pain than any heated argument they'd ever had. He was more popular than any premier league football star: a man's man, and a woman's dream. He was conscious of his appeal and felt it his obligation to please as many single, lonely women that could sustain his fickle interest. Infidelity, in their relationship, was like a wound that never quite healed. And more than two years of enduring endless affairs was taking its toll on Claudia.

Her mother had warned her. There was something about men who wore earrings that made Mrs Bennett feel uncomfortable. Men who liked women's things made her feel suspicious. 'Next thing you know, the man will be wearing your baggies!' she often laughed. Claudia didn't see the joke. Her mother had been instinctively correct about her choice of men before and it always disturbed her.

She looked at her watch. It was twenty to nine. She looked at the phone.

He's probably at Cairo's.

It was Russell's regular Friday night haunt and the place where they'd originally met, one raucous Friday night while she celebrated Leah's birthday with their usual circle of friends. Russell was a friend of Leah's brother Phillip – the two had worked together at BT before Russell had moved on to manage a mobile phone shop. Leah had made it clear from the beginning that she was not impressed with her pal's choice. Although she couldn't deny his physical attractiveness he had more than a penchant for dancers and actresses, and to her, that made him fickle and immature. She respected her friends decision to go out with him and gradually developed an uncomfortable liking for his spirit, but she kept her distance when she could, and picked up the pieces when he tore at Claudia's world with his macho indiscretions.

It was ten past nine when Claudia finally surrendered to temptation and phoned Russell's mobile. It was switched off.

The bastard she thought. Phones were his thing, and his silver Nokia was rarely off. Russell was too scared to miss business. I doubt he's at home.

She rang anyway, and was surprised to find it engaged. Russell at home on a Friday night was an unusual occurrence. If he wasn't working late, tidying accounts at the shop, he would predictably be at Cairo's, or with her. But lately Claudia had noticed an alteration in habit and mood, a pattern she'd seen before. It unnerved her.

Claudia stared at the portable television and listened to the news. After a few minutes she tried Russell's number again. Still engaged. She was puzzled, and to distract herself decided to take Leah up on her offer. Maybe a girl's night out was what she needed. She dialled the Tottenham number but got the answer machine. She's still at the gym, Claudia smiled to herself, which is probably where I should be...

An hour later and Russell's phone was still engaged. The suspense was beating her up like a mismatched boxer in a title fight. There was only one way to be sure...

Armed with a sense of purpose, and a brewing temper, Claudia jumped in her Peugeot and drove towards Stoke Newington. Oblivious to the fact that she'd sped through a red light and near-missed a pedestrian on a zebra crossing, she weaved through her favoured shortcut to Russell's house. The local radio station's love zone had just begun and the stream of gushy ballads caused tears to glaze her eyes. She hit the metal button to turn the radio off.

Who would it be this time? Some wannabe model? Another woman six years younger, four inches taller and two shades lighter? A white woman? What if she got it wrong and embarrassed herself again, like the time she screamed at him at the gym when she'd found him talking to a woman that turned out to be his cousin? If there is someone else, will she drop him for good, or take him back for the umpteenth predictable time? Would Leah give up on her, as she always threatened, if she let Russell get away with one more liberty?

The black Saab 900 was parked outside Number 37. Russell had to be in. A dim light glowed through the muslin curtains of the living room, and upstairs looked dark and unoccupied. Claudia parked in an empty space on the opposite side of the cul de sac. She pulled the key from the car door and tugged her jacket straight while pausing on the pavement. In her haste she'd buttoned it unevenly. Her body felt moist under her silk blouse. Beads of sweat had appeared on her upper lip and she suddenly felt lost and awkward. This time no sorry excuses or cheap apologies would suffice. She'd been pushed to the limit and was about to end two years and four months of internal turmoil.

Ditching Russell was something Claudia's temper, not her heart, had toyed with in the past. She'd allowed him to get away with casual affairs, justifying them in her head as "just sex." Even rumours of a child younger than their relationship had been cast aside as jealousy. While her other friends had given up even discussing his philandering ways, Leah listened and absorbed Claudia's excuses and self denial like an attentive student. Russell, however, had often told his woman that her best friend's tough exterior simply masked her insecurity. That, or she was a dyke. Male logic.

At the front door she could hear music through the glass pane: mellow, smooth and seductive. Her suspicions intensified. Instead of ringing the bell, Claudia pounded her fist against the panelled wooden door and stood back. There was no reply. She banged again.

When seconds began to feel like minutes she opted for long piercing rings on the doorbell. The hallway suddenly illuminated, injecting a rapid surge of nervous energy through her. Claudia took a couple of paces backwards and folded her arms defensively.

'Who is it?' Russell shouted from behind the panelled door. He sounded irritated and it unnerved her even more.

She responded in a similar fashion, 'It's me!'

'Who the hell's me?' came the fiery response.

The fact that he didn't recognise her voice stunned her. She didn't reply, but stared at the door as Russell appeared sheepishly, and half-asleep from behind it.

'Oh hi babes. What's happening?' He leaned his half-naked torso against the side of the door and yawned like a righteous lion. 'Did you get my message? I called you.'

'Aren't you going to let me in?'

'Not if you're going to give me grief. I told you I was checking the guys later and I'm tired, so I'm just resting before I chip. Listen, go home and I'll check you tomorrow.' He stretched his neck forward like a giraffe, in an attempt to place a kiss on her vexed lips. Claudia pulled back.

'Now listen to me good, you fucker. I don't give a shit about the guys. You're not going to get away with treating me like this anymore. I want to talk to you and I don't give a damn how tired you are, I'm not having this conversation on the bloody street. You may be a fucking lowlife, but I'm not. I'm sick of...'

'Now listen to me and listen to me good,' he responded, his voice softer and more controlling in an attempt to prevent nosy neighbours being drawn to the drama outside his house. 'Don't fucking come and start cursing outside my house, Claudia. If you want to argue go and find one of your pussy friends to fight with, me na into dat. Me tired and me na have time fe dis.'

Claudia knew she had wound him up now. Russell only ever switched to dialect when he was vex. He began to close the door, but Claudia mustered every ounce of will in her frame and pushed past him. As she stormed into his living room, he kicked the front door shut with his right leg and pursued her at speed.

She stood in the centre of the room beside a glass table. Streams of tears made tracks through her foundation as if marking the paths for trails of mascara to follow. The salty pools rested on her top lip. She licked them away with the tip of her tongue.

'What is it with you Claudia?'

She fought to respond but the words were wedged in the pit of her throat. She swallowed and tried in vain to reply.

'I'm... you can't do this to... why are you treating me...'

Before she could finish she crumpled to the floor deflated. Her face now moist with sweat, tears and snot had transformed from arrogant to pathetic.

Russell watched, temporarily confused, then took slow, cautious steps towards her like a gamekeeper approaching a just-sedated beast. He placed a firm palm on the centre of her arched back, and after several feeble attempts to slap him away, Claudia surrendered to his calming strokes. She drew in deep breaths as he pacified her.

Minutes passed. As he cupped her cheeks and lifted her head

to gain eye contact she fought against him pushing down with her chin to bury her smudged features in to her chest. But Russell lowered his head to meet her eyes and smiled that youthful, seductive smile that often said more for than words ever could. Like a father teasing a spoilt child he played with expressions in an attempt to steal a smile. It eventually worked.

'Look at your face, man!' he laughed as he wiped her eyes.

Claudia raised the back of her sleeve to complete the job and dried her face. 'What do you work yourself up like this for?'

She was silent as he cradled her in his arms and rocked her to the sound of Maxwell. The room, with its eggshell walls and modern furniture was serene. Claudia remained placid as she rested between Russell's legs on the floor, wrapped in his arms.

But his mind was agitated.

You can't go on like this man he thought to himself. You've got to sort this shit out.

But sorting out his shit had always proved a difficult task. His spirit commanded constant stimulation and no matter how much he was into a woman, he could never resist temptation. As he shifted his body to get comfortable, he noticed the zip of his jeans were half down and remembered he'd been lying on his bed upstairs.

Through her hazy vision Claudia looked up at Russell and smiled meekly. He kissed her forehead with light touches of his lips and made his way down towards her mouth until their tongues massaged each other in an intense kiss. The throbbing in her head soon gave way to a throbbing between her legs. How could she give up a man who stirred her so? She raised her body and wrapped both arms around his neck, pulling his weight on top of her as she lowered herself to the floor.

He pressed his erect tool against her pelvic bone and kissed her neck in the way he knew she loved. She wriggled like a worm daubed in salt and before long was dizzy with passion as he filled her collapsed body with life. Claudia was back in her comfort zone.

Russell meanwhile was aware that he'd put her back there. Seduction worked every time. With Claudia... with Carol... with Kate... with Iona...

...and with Leah, who lay silent and scared in Russell's bed upstairs.

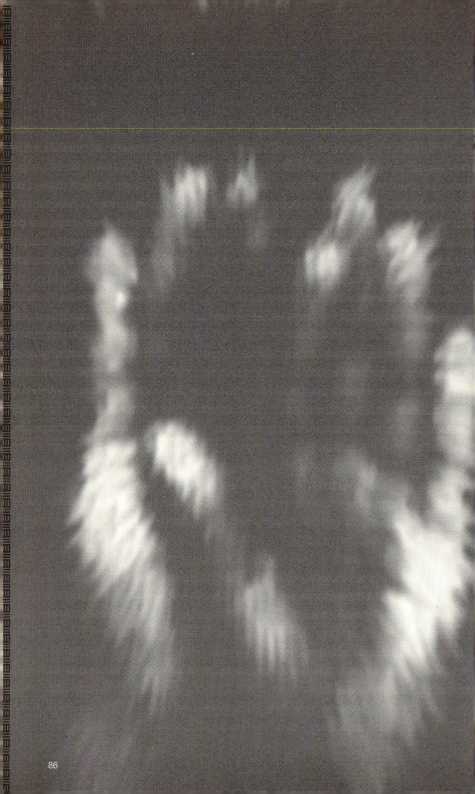

Crates
Joanna Traynor

Cheryl cannot swim through an ocean of words. Words that lap back and forth. Words that can be paddled in. Words in a bay somewhere. Any bay or coastline. Cheryl cannot swim or even paddle. She only knows the words that have come inland. Their sound. She does not have horizons. She doesn't see the words coming, and after drowning she doesn't know she's drowned. She would like to see as far as they can see. The words that she can't see, she knows – just as sure as Christopher Columbus knew – are just a journey away.

Cheryl lives in a crate among crates. Through the strips of plywood, daylight casts her life across the floor and she compares what she has, with him across the way. He is not in today. But that does not make his box empty. No. On the contrary. It is nearly full. Where on earth is the space to move? In his crate every strip of plywood is covered in colour or metal. Patterns. Patterns that won't be reshaped. Patterns he has bought in. He wears patterns. And when Cheryl goes out, to pick up food, she sees the same patterns repeated in place after space. Sometimes she thinks she has discovered a new pattern but so sooner has she treasured that rarity – there is another one, and then another one. The man across the way has a crate full of patterns. She has a treasure chest in her head, full of dreams and rarities.

Treasure chests are for pirates and in her time she's had a few. A pirate took her kid away. Gave her a couple, too, but they never grew. Now she is raped of beauty by the need to survive. The need to keep looking for a reason to sleep peacefully. There is always a reason for fits in the crates. Everybody gets fits in the crates. What is the key to peaceful sleep? She wonders. Dreaming virtual jewels for the treasure chest. Jewels no one can steal.

If Cheryl had a horizon she might see what was coming. The television is not a horizon. It tells her what to wear and says what is coming on at the pictures. It tells her what car she could drive if she were a millionaire, for surely there are millionaires out there? She'd like to meet one. She thinks she sees them when she's sat on the bus. She sees them tapping their fingers on steering wheels, typing out secret codes as they wait for the lights to change; for new horizons to spring up on the windscreen of their lives. In town she can see them in restaurants, with their elbows on the table laughing. Laughing at their parents for daring to tell them that such behaviour is bad manners. And Cheryl feels bad mannered walking past them. Watching them raise spoons of soup to their mouths. She's embarrassed. She is walking through their bathroom almost. She might be watching them shit as they cram bread rolls through their shiny, soggy lips that tear at the bread as though it were flesh. She wonders that they allow her to walk the pavements – allow her to watch. She is gone before their eyes say she is next. Before she becomes the second course of their meal. And she sees them jump in to taxis, out of the light, like vampires. She sees them, but never meets them.

Sometimes she listens to the radio. It tells her to buy carpets or blares boys, like wind-up toys they are, singing songs that remind her of nursery rhymes electrified. The radio gets a life of its own, and like a chained up dog, howls from its space; howls of anger because it is trapped in the corner of the room, and the noise of the carpet man raps on her skull until she knows where to buy her carpet from. The blaring and damaging noise tears at her brain, tears her away from the dream that would have her meet a man on a bridge. A bridge that is lit up by sprinkles of tinkle lights. And rocks, like a hammock, in the still summer air. So she can dream all this, she turns the radio off soon after.

Sometimes the door bell rings. It is always rung by the shape of a head that bobs from side to side in frosted glass. The bobbing head is nervous for it is standing on a precipice, firm but not sturdy, constructively balanced to precision. Still it is a precipice. If any disorder should crescend in a minute or a month, the crate could send a mattress through a window or a child down the stairs or a woman on the game. The insides would come out. Windows are smashed and glass cuts to the ground in grey piles of sand that might be boiled sweets not wanted and everywhere. The precipice of the crate is vulnerable to the silent jump of an athlete with a flick knife, a flaring nose of desire with the advantage of surprise and knowledge of the territory. The crates are corridored for rats to maze the stranger with the claws of a hammer, corner him with smells to warn of further terror, guide him as a sacrifice from some other world. To Cheryl's crate.

She sees the bobbing head and wonders who has taken to mounting the stairs labelled *I white knight of the city* and *I mad professor of the hood*. Who has been paid to snarl at the urined ghetto of her crate? Who has sacrificed safety to crush glass with man-made soles, to take the stairs two at a time, looking forward and back in search of a crime upon themselves?

It will be charity. It will be a policeman. The SS. Or neighbourhood watchman. It will be a catalogue girl. A thief. It will be the lecky man. It will be someone lost, in the wrong quadrangle, in the wrong block, crate and place. At the wrong time. So watch it. After nine, it's not the time to open the door to bobbing heads in the corridor.

There's another man next door, who Cheryl can't see. He plays music. Morning and evening. He plays reggae music so loud it is in her own flat, it is so loud. But she does not mind because it swallows the place. The beat helps her heart to beat. It swallows her whole mind and she has a list in her head of the tunes that she likes. Not a named list. A tune list. She has the first few bars written to her brain like a catechism. If she had the words she might go next door and make a request, but she only knows the tunes and cannot sing or hum melodies, out loud and alone. At the weekends it's fairly quiet because the man is out then. He takes his music with him. Everywhere he goes. Men come and drag big boxes up and down the stairs at the weekend. During the week is beat time for Cheryl and she likes it. She signed a petition to say that she didn't. She was scared of the people with the pen. And she wanted to prove she could write her name. So the man next door wouldn't talk anymore and only raised the volume higher and higher, and she used the beat to exercise her flabby thighs and stomach that corrugated her flesh into folds that were sore.

She can't watch the television on such nights for the screen of images only charges at the waves of the beat in the air. Bellows like a nazi. It can't beat the beat. Except for the soaps. She must hear the soaps and luckily the man with the music, he likes the soaps, too. Soap knits her existence into an existence. It is not a hell in her crate when the soap makes a mirror of her life, and says that all is right with the world for look, it is here on tv for everyone to see. It is not a hell at all. It's the way it is.

Cheryl wants to be a teacher. She knows teachers. She remembers them. She has set her mind to it. She is to go to college to learn reading and writing. That will be a start. She reads very little. Very slowly. She can write her name and words like sun, tree, hat, dog and cat. But she can see pictures better. She likes pictures so maybe she can teach art but the man down the job search says she must learn to read and write before she can teach art and while she doesn't see the whole sense of this, she believes him. The man is gentle with her and fills out the forms at the college. Someone will help her. She must enrol and the word enrol makes her feel rounded, whole. She is, at last, going to be on something round. Rolling somewhere. And she must choose between cigarettes or bus fare.

On the bus she is glad no smoking is allowed. It quells the panging to resignation. It makes her feel like she's contributing something. She sits upstairs. For to sit downstairs is to say one is scared of life or too old for it. To sit downstaris and miss out on the view across the dual carriageways is to say one's life is even smaller than it really is. To sit in the dark and say no to the sunshine is to say one has given up. Is to be afraid.

Cheryl is in strides off the bus and is beginning the rest of her life. She believes she must pretend these things to get through all the truth of it. She is nearly at the college but has to sit on a bench first. She must go through her reasoning again, understand exactly why she is there. Why she is able and willing to make a fool of herself, admit to, submit to all those people who say she is a dunce. She remembers school. Her page of black inky marks that the teacher put a red line through – and handed right back. Then he packed his case with homework from all the other kids and went home. Instead of rising from the bench and running home herself she makes that memory the reason to stay. The memory is an old one. This was a new day. No longer would that homework kick her in the teeth. The job search man made her think that way. Think positively, he said. Christopher Columbus thought the earth was flat. And like any lie, the more she practiced thinking it, the more she began to believe that the new world was just a journey away. The truth was no longer a string to cling onto, to be led by, to breathe by. Truth does not bring joy, just as silence does not bring peace.

From the bench she watched the rich go past in cars and the buses groan after, in anger and impatience. She watched pushchairs withstand kerbs and babes withstand the bouncing. Shops for sale. Shops for sale. Children on skateboards nearly die. She was joined in this watch by a man who sat too close to be anonymous. Too close to be his own self, so she looked in his face and strange it was. A difference. A silence. A longing in his eyes. A white long beard. A red velvet dress and shoes to bear an elf not the giant that he was.

I am not beautiful says Cheryl to herself, used to pick-up men with pick-up lines. She was old enough to know she wasn't worthy anymore, the boil of youth lanced and dried up. But strange, no pick-up line was sent to waft under her nose like a jeer, a snidy cock at her. And yet he wasn't truly silent. Under his

arm, a sketch pad and he pulls it out as if to identify himself. She sees flashes of faces across the pad and before she can think of a goodbye he is sketching her anger across the page in a cartoon of charcoal. As if deaf and dumb and almost crying he lashes out the images of his head, frantic to reproduce. A camera eye developing her in seconds. A mass of power burst through the end of his stick, sent by the energy frothing through his snuffles of excitement, the pinching of his lips, the determination of his thought. And his power holds her there, in permanence, on paper,
on the bench.

The giant artist filled in the forms for her. She knew someone would. The man in the job search said so. Then she is out in the sun, walking in a glide, alongside his red dress and quietened mind.

The Maryland Gallery by the canal, cheered itself up with broken shards of stained red glass, stabbing at the stone and industry of long ago. No windows. Locked. This was his home, he said. He called his home a gallery. A gallery. Only certain people know of it – he has no wish to be public. He shall be recognized after his death. He couldn't bear to see people before then, or for people to see him. And she remembered. Of course. Hadn't she heard that before. Death is the sacrifice of the true artist. The name of the place made Cheryl feel safe.

Up straight steps and then round and round a spiral staircase. She follows the hem of his dress, watching it drag its way through the soil of his living. She pretends disinterest, like a bride arranged with a groom from another world. She is so small to be climbing so high she thinks. And sliding away, a wood panelled door he shifts through it. He beckons her to follow him. And then. There! The glass sky roof is shaped like the point of a pencil and the light from it shafts her, raises her mind up further and higher than even the virtual scapes of her hardest dreams. The circular horizon of sky applauds her. The clapping of the wind against the glass shatters her head, to make her twitch this way and that. It is painful to see as far as the eye can see – so she stopped. She hooded her eyes to the sky. Almost frightened now. She looked up from her feet to all around her. The walls of the gallery were carpeted canvases of painted pain on faces she has seen before but can't recognize. His images were laughing at her. And now she laughed back. A frayed laugh. A panic laugh. A fit. A fit of fear. His images mirrored her dreams. She was afriad now that her dreams were real. And, of course, she felt a surge of gladness. She laughed. She held her belly for laughs and then more laughs. And then slowed, breathed quietly. Fell down. Exhausted. Fot it was the longest journey of her life, following this giant to his sanctum. His treasure chest. His sky.

'You', he said, passing her a pillow. 'You, my dear, are a rarity.'

A Good Buy
Yinka Sunmonu

You don't forget significant events. Take life with my husband Tan – the studmuffin. I met him in a supermarket. At aisle seventeen to be exact, beside the chilled cabinet. He had a well-stocked basket of vegetables, fruit, Häagen Dazs ice cream and a few bottles of vintage wines. I recall that he was meticulous in rearranging his purchases, eyeing me as he did so. He had such presence that there was no need to really scrutinise his goods. You knew his type – fresh, calm, self assured and confident.

Life was always good with Tan. He qualified as a chartered surveyor and then became preoccupied with property speculation, keeping a close analysis on Land Registry figures to determine where we ought to be living. He was always good at building his life and mine. It was his suggestion to move to the golden triangle near Bath, a new hotspot, so that we could show our friends we had truly arrived. He planned to stay in London to study for his Masters in business administration and come down to see me at weekends. I refused to go, because in between his constructive planning he hadn't included a creative design of his own – a baby.

They say that some men panic when they are told of impending fatherhood, but not Tan. He went out into the garden to build a playground. And then it happened. He invited me on to the confessional.

It's ironic that they're showing the programme today. There's time to watch it before the match begins, but there is no need. It's repeated in my mind for the barrenness that my life has become. I've even timed it to the last second...

I am standing in the hospitality room with the heat bearing down on me. Five minutes pass. I feel sticky and the palms of my hands are soaking wet. I ask myself if I am doing the right thing by agreeing to appear on *The Show*. What kind of nutter goes forward to humiliate themselves in public? And then I receive my answer... because everybody wants their five minutes of fame and you want yours. Maybe I did.

I pace up and down in the room and then I stop to pour myself some tomato juice. Nervously, I miss my mouth and curse for staining my blouse, even though I'll be able to hide it by buttoning my cardigan.

I start to read some trashy magazines, but I'm suddenly not interested in dirt. A minute has passed. Nobody comes and I am still alone with my thoughts. It's not too late to quit, I say, and on stepping towards the door, they call me. I pause... then I die for a microsecond, floating into the arms of two assistants in black suits who transport me in the lift down to the ground floor. Struggling in my body-fitted cardigan, I'm being committed.

They push me back gently as the star of *The Show* walks

forward, and looks the same in real life as he does on the television but with one exception, he is taller than I expected him to be. He turns and holds his hand out to a make-up artist who buffs his nails, and I laugh. It's his temples that need the brush-up. I want to move forward to check out the grey matter but I'm too slow. They are announcing him, the star of *The Show*.

The audience shouts out three times and starts to whoop. I hear myself praying while hopeless sounds ride the sullen air. Suddenly my head is spinning... ready, ready, ready.

Let's bring her in.

Suddenly I am on the stage in front of hundreds of glaring people, who applaud me. I grow suspicious.

How is your relationship?

He wants me to talk about Tan and I feel myself animated. Our baby kicks inside me and I want to speak for him, let him know how much his father treasures me. For that is how it has always been and how it is meant to be and so I start, 'We've been married for eight years. He's... '

The crowd gasp and my mouth sets. I ease it open to finish my sentence. 'It was fine till I got here.' I make sure my body is taut as I speak and that I maintain eye contact with the star.

... now you know that you're here to be told something.

I hear these words, 'Mya, you know I love you...'

I shake saying, 'Cut the niceties Tan and get to the part these people want to stand up for.'

I scan the audience, watching their faces, watching me. They clap again believing I have control.

'I don't know how to tell you this... '

My body twitches. I'm frightened. My baby performs a rugby tackle on me. I'm scared. I've missed something because out comes this monkfish woman prancing about on the stage, pointing a finger and throwing colourful language in my face.

'Black-eyed bitch,' she is chanting. 'I'm his pleasure now, and you're just stale routine, get it?'

Tan is fast-talking now. He's had an affair. A one night stand. He says it only happened twice or thrice, that she stalks him. But I don't understand the stories. He's telling me that she's as versatile as a mixed-use leisure complex, and that he checked in because he couldn't juggle the pressures of work and an unborn baby.

She, the woman, is called Gloria. She's a disgrace to her name, there is nothing glorious about her. The honey-coloured face does not match the ebonyed neck. She throws her head back, laughing, telling me to return to the convent or learn my trade. 'He wants this, morning noon and night.' She stands up and twirls, but I'm not looking, oh gory, Gloria.

The audience is singing – pressure, pressure, pressure… treasure, treasure, treasure. I hear them and it's true. I have become his pressure not his treasure, but I won't cry. I'm concentrating so hard on preventing the tears that I know will fall as worthless stones that I no longer hear what the woman is saying. I see her in the supermarket. Her basket contains refried beans, twice-baked potatoes and duck. For dessert she takes profiteroles.

The audience is waiting for me to speak. I only have eyes for her. She reeks of Calvin Klein's Contradiction. Every gram of fat is tucked into those D&G trousers, and the Katherine Hamnett top screams from physical abuse. As she smiles I see the gap in her yellow pronged teeth and then she starts to dig her clawed nails into Tan, making a tiny imprint that will become permanent.

My eyes are flaming fire and I'm exhibiting some kind of brutal strength and she stands there. She's compost, sprinkling herself over my man, and they're soul mates for Tan is wearing the Contradiction I bought him to celebrate our anniversary yesterday.

This Gloria opens a pocket mirror and starts shaking her coarse mane, running her fingers through it. It's then that I see the thin rows close to her scalp. I hold her gaze. Then I lift up my hand and place it in my scalp, forking through my hair, lifting it, rubbing it until I cover the long length that is all mine. Psyche.

She's not all that. If she possesses basic literacy and numeracy certificates I would give her my home, but I, like the supporters I suddenly have in the audience, can see she relies on mud, and hair at £1.99 a bundle.

'And why not?' she asks baiting the crowd, 'I always aim to please.'

I hear the hisses. The angry retorts on my behalf. I'm grateful.

Gloria is raising a hand to lift her top. We have now reached *The Show's* summit, where they place that moveable blur on the television to block out the salacious parts. I cannot and will not retaliate as I place a hand on the resting place of my love-child. Despite my discomfort, I look at what she has to display – chocolate buttons – and I'm embarrassed for this cheap piece of skirt.

I turn my head towards Tan who is sitting, grasping the sides of the chair as if facing execution. He cannot face me. By the time he turns to me, it's too late. My eyes are focused on the floor, working out how much this day is costing me. Too much for somebody in my position.

Talk to her, says the host.

He does not know that my decision is made.

Talk to him. Could you forgive one indiscretion?

He does not realise that he cannot bait me, that I won't help improve the ratings.

Hold on, he says, feeding from my silence. *Tan, haven't you more to say?*

I see the sides of his mouth upturn into a sly smile. I return to the supermarket. In the metallic basket, matching his temples, the star holds a large bowl, olive oil, lemons and chillies. He has no drinks, but I imagine him to get high on cocktails.

Tan fills the seat. Although he has nothing to say, his attitude appears too casual. I want to stand up and spit the mucus at the back of my throat in his face, but then I notice he's becoming restless and I settle for that. Hah! He's not coping well. His intelligent quotient and sparkling wit is disappearing fast and at each interlude his demeanour, that air of cool, is being replaced by a flounder out of its depths. The studio heat is making his moustache limp, sweat is streaming down the sides of his face, he is flouncing.

'Be a man,' I tell him as he flaps. 'I can take what you have to say.'

'Well, I've been studying real hard.'

'Yeah, right, by getting yourself pork scratchings on the side.'

'Listen to you, Miss Chicken Dinner. No wonder he's so starved.' Gloria interrupts.

'At least he was coming home to a superior cut, and not spare ribs or chump chops.'

I hear the roar and I really want to bow. Gloria jumps from her chair, holds up a platform sandal and starts to lurch forward.

Now you know that quiet people are dangerous people and nobody makes a fool of me. I pick up my chair and say, 'Come and get a roasting if you want it that much.'

The crowd is on edge clapping their eager hands and yelling the host's name, a constant, rhythmic reminder of where I am. They want action. I see them holding bread knives. My blood is curdling and I want action. I'm going to kill that worthless hog, not because of Tan, who I hope trips over the electrical cables when he leaves the studio, but because of the humiliation I've been caused on national tv. I can't stop thinking of all the people who know me and those who didn't but do now… Mya, Mya, Mya.

The star speaks: *We don't want you to get excited now with the baby and all but if...*

He shuts up and looks off balance as I sit down, accepting his words of wisdom and concern. Oh yes, I watched the show with the woman about to drop triplets. One episode is enough.

Tan says he still cares. Now comes the laughter, the jeers convicting me of suck-holing if I ever contemplate 'another try'.

'He's got you on a string,' a suited brother points out. 'He's the one who deserves to be on a leash. A dog's one.'

I clap for him as rapturous giggles echo in the studio.

The star says *we're running out of time, although he can take one more comment.*

'Lady, if you don't recognise when you're being played, you're better off back in the convent. Better still, live life a little. Let me show you, p–l–e–a–s–e.'

I go red with embarrassment and turn my face away as members of the audience drum their feet and a few women scream.

Tan shifts position, ever so slightly, and I catch him looking at the cosmetic filly. Still he has nothing to say. There's a brief flicker in his eyes that reminds me of a look I've seen before. I strain to think. It's animal heat. The type contained in bull dogs who raise their hind legs indiscriminately. How divine. I hate him.

I'm parched. I drink my saliva greedily and pray I can get off stage soon.

My baby is kicking me. I sense he's frustrated as I feel a sudden pain. I fall to the floor, writhing in agony.

'She'll do anything to keep you,' yells Gloria. 'Tell her how you're planning to dump her once she's in Bath.'

My waters break. Do something, please. I'm ready, ready, ready. I'm begging, pleading, pushing the ratings with each uncontractural thrust.

The heat from the cameras intensify. There is great light. I hear applause, music. I smell blood and somebody switches everything off.

When I awake, I'm alone in a hospital bed. Mothers are with their cots. I don't have one. The doctor says there was a problem with the umbilical cord, giver and feeder of life.

I lament because Tan and I no longer have life to give. Days pass. Weeks. I do not talk, will not cry, even though they tell me that it is best to grieve. I want my own time and space, away from the public domain.

I start a daily pilgrimage to the supermarket and gradually begin to find comfort in helping other women make the right selection. You can tell a lot by checking out what people have in their trolleys or baskets. Looking back, could Tan's selection of fruit and veg have whispered any clues?

I feel so grounded that I may open the Mya Hart International Food Shopology Centre for the unsuspected. It could net me a fortune and when it does, I'm going to treat myself to a trip to Paris, *le cité d'amour*, on Eurostar. Life is for living.

Gloriously, I trudge upstairs to have a bath. I wallow in the cool water and suddenly salt tears rain on my pool of dreams.

The Negative
Norma Pollock

I couldn't let him in. I could tell from his cruel grey eyes that he wanted to summon up the beast in me. That primitive croak of ecstasy that both startled and terrified me twenty years ago. Seymour had been the devil to lay there with no clothes on, hands behind his head and let me take him.

I shut the door in the plumber's face. The Council would have to send someone else to unblock the toilet. Someone who'd been neutered. Mr Fisher should have known better and was in for an earful of abuse for sending me a sex maniac. I may look like a spring chicken with my hair in two plaits and my ankle socks, but I'm 44 years old. You see black skin ages well, and I've had no pickney to tear up my belly or cause me aggravation, and no husband, thank God.

I don't leave the flat unless I have to. Not that there is anywhere special to go. In the summer I visit Auntie Millie in Dalston, but it's winter now so auntie has to visit me. She never married either. She gets on my tits at times, but I really don't know what I'd do without her.

It's not safe out there, believe me. Everywhere you go there're men who want to stick their thing in your mouth or inside your body. It's disgusting. Like that Mr Thomas in the flat below. He thinks he is clever, but I know what he's up to. He can see up my skirt as I walk across his ceiling, and when I'm in the bath I get very nervous knowing that he's staring straight up my privates.

When I've dressed, I bang on the floor with the mop and curse Mr Thomas and his family. Going to the toilet is even worse. I have to put newspaper down the bowl to stop Mr Thomas from seeing me perform my bodily functions.

His wife came to my door the other day. A very nice woman, too, a fellow Jamaican, but she doesn't know what her husband is like because she's blinded by love. She's got no excuse but her monthly to stop her old man from poking her every minute of the day and night, and even then I bet he doesn't mind it getting dipped in blood. Probably turns him on more. But me I'm not having none of it. No, sir. Not from him, or anyone. I'll leave that to the likes of Mrs Thomas.

I listened to what she had to say about how it was making herself and her husband ill, all the noise and accusations. She even returned the letters I sent her, explaining the things that her husband did behind her back. She said it was all filth and she's right; all men are animals.

Recently I have taken to writing to Mr Fisher at the council to see what he can do about Mr Thomas, as the situation is getting out of hand. He'll have to move. You see I have started to get sensations down below. I even went to see young Doctor Marks, because he is handsome and at least listens to me, not like his old man. He scribbled out a letter for me to take to the Hackney Hospital Psychiatric Department, but there's nothing wrong with my head. It's Mr Thomas's fingers moving inside my knickers.

It doesn't just happen in the flat. It happens when I'm out shopping or sitting on the bus. All of a sudden the sensations come and I start to squirm in my seat or on the spot, if I'm standing. It is a very uncomfortable and distressing feeling. People are starting to look at me funny and move away from me if they can. I shout out, 'Stop it Mr Thomas. Stop it. Leave me alone. Get your hand from out of there!' But he doesn't listen. He's too busy trying to summon up the beast in me, but it won't happen that way.

It's true that Mr Thomas doesn't look well the few times I spied him from my balcony recently. He may be younger than me, but is big and walks kind of stiff, like his thing is giving him trouble.

Our paths rarely cross. I know his movements and he's not one for going out of an evening. You see he can't bear to be away from me. I'm his entertainment. Even when he's poking his wife, he looks up hoping to snatch a glimpse of me undressing.

There's been a lot of wailing and movement in the flat below in the past few days. I overheard one of my neighbours telling another that Mr Thomas had died of a heart attack.

Magically, my sensations stopped after that. I now have the urge to rip off all my clothes, once the curtains have been drawn of an afternoon. I no longer have to bang on the floor with the mop or shove newspaper down the toilet. Mr Thomas cannot see me any more. I've been liberated.

Outside is another matter. There are still plenty of men out there to be wary of but I know who they are and avoid them at all costs.

I bumped into Mrs Thomas and one of her daughters as I was leaving the local greengrocer shop the day after her husband's funeral. She stood in front of me and asked if I was happy now. I told her I was feeling much better lately. Then like a woman possessed, Mrs Thomas grabbed hold of my throat and spat out a jumble of foul insults. Her daughter prised her mother's fingers from around my neck, crying out that I wasn't worth it, that I was sick. This comment hurt me more than being choked.

Coughing, I picked up my two potatoes from the road and hurried home. I had a desperate urge to pee and undress at the same time. I did both in the bathroom, then hobbled into the bedroom carrying my bundle of clothes in front of me.

As I reached out to pull the curtains, I heard a deep masculine sigh. I screamed and dropped everything. Trembling, I turned around slowly and gasped. Lying stretched out on my bed was no other than Mr Thomas, alive and well and naked. His hands were behind his head and his huge thing perked at the sight of my bare body. He was all flesh and I should have found it obscene, but for the way he looked at me. His eyes were big and brown and seemed to draw me towards him. They said, Take me, take me. I'm all yours now.

It was happening again, just like with Seymour twenty years ago, and how could I resist him, or the call of the beast.

A Suitable Candidate
Dorothy Koomson

I look at my watch and, without meaning to, sigh. A deep, heavy, weight-of-the-world-on-my-shoulders type of sigh. Still 45 minutes and 15 seconds, no, 14, no, 13, no 12, seconds to go. Not that I'm counting or anything. I look at the chipped cup of tea in front of me to avoid looking at my watch. I'm counting and that's winding me up. Why does time go so slowly sometimes? Last night I woke up about five times to check the time, to check I hadn't overslept, to see if it was time to get up yet. And each time I looked at the three alarm clocks by my bed (each set to go off within 10 minutes of each other) time seemed to be going backwards. I'd eventually gotten up an hour before any of the clocks went off and sat watching *Sesame Street* with a growing fear that I was going to spend the rest of my life like that: sat at home watching telly on my own.

I'd applied for a position on a large northern newspaper. And I want this job. I really want this job. Since I'd opened the letter inviting me to the interview I'd thought of little else. What am I talking about? I'd thought of nothing else. No one knows how much I want this job. It would mean no one could tell me I was rubbish or second-rate anymore. I'd had enough of that with Jason. How the hell did he get into my head? It's not like I was totally in love with him or anything. It's not like I was going to marry him or anything. It's not like he totally destroyed any confidence or trust I had in myself or the whole of the human race, or anything. Well, no more. Once I get this job no one could tell me a damn thing because all that slaving away I did on the local paper in the outer Hebrides would've been worth it. I could stop all that mad commuting I had to do. And I'd get a pay rise so I can actually afford to buy some stuff for my flat. You know, some carpet or at least some rugs so I won't have to play How Far Can I Hop? each morning across the nice, but cold, wood floors. Saucepans would be nice, too. There's only so much takeaway and microwave food a girl can survive on. And furniture, could I do with some furniture. A chair, a bean bag, a bed, a coffee table and, of course, my TV are all I took when I left Jason. When I think the name my mind's natural defences kick in and I force my train of thought back to what is ahead. Back to what is now the most important thing in my life.

I'd worked for my shot at this position. I deserved it. I'd have climbed over several people to get that position. Well, not really, because I'd been brought up right, but I'd give it a good try. A damn good try. But anyway, the fact that I'd got an interview meant I was, at least on paper, a suitable candidate.

Unconsciously, I shift in my seat. This skirt is a little tighter around the waist than when I'd last tried it on. And I'm a little worried my rather magnificent, well, okay, large breasts will pop off one of the buttons on my shirt or jacket, or both before I've actually sat down in the interview room – or worse, as I sit down in the interview room. Just don't think about it, I say in my head. You're going to get this job.

I'd got into town a bit too early and had found this cafe just around the corner from the place of my interview. I'd arrived early because I didn't want to be held up by traffic or cancelled trains or non-existent buses. It's mid-autumn. Brown leaves, shorter days, cooler air. And because it's autumn I know that even a hint of a leaf falling anywhere near a train line or road will cause the whole of Leeds to grind to a halt. But despite my refusal to have my travel plans scotched by the weather, I'm beginning to wish I'd stayed at home a bit longer.

I look briefly around the small cafe. Only a handful of other people sit in here with me: two are staring out of the window; two others stare into their cups of tea. They're breaking up, I realise. I know those looks well. Far too well.

I could kill for a cigarette right now. Even though I've given up. It's been six of the longest days of my life. I've taken to wearing gloves when I watch TV. I used to chain smoke in front of the telly and because I can't smoke, I'd started biting my nails instead. Only wearing the blue woollen winter gloves would stop me biting my fingers off with my nails. Shame I'd started to develop a penchant for wool…

I jump when the bell behind the door jangles and five lads stumble in, laughing and talking loudly. I look up at them as they joke and jostle each other on the way to the counter. My eyes flick over them. White boys in pin-striped suits. Nothing new in this part of town. And neither is their attitude. Arrogant and carefree. They all give the woman behind the counter a hard time because, unfortunately for her, she's made an effort with her appearance. Well, I say effort. My eyes flick over her, too. She's bleached her hair to within an inch of its life and obviously applied her pinky-range foundation with a trowel. Her clothes are about five sizes too small. And let's not even go there with her mascara. Dead shrivelled spiders look better. Jeez, I feel sorry for her. Poor little blonde girl. Not only is she a walking, talking fashion and make-up disaster, she's also enjoying the snide and sarcastic comments the group of lads are making. She thinks they like her. The girl has no idea. No idea at all. I have to avert my eyes, for fear of having to intervene. I can't watch cruelty to animals and not do something.

I take a sip of tea but hold it in my mouth because it's the foulest thing I've tasted. Ever. That's how come it's lasted 37 minutes. It tastes so foul, I can only manage little sips every now and then. I swallow when my only other option is to spit it back into the cup The tea should be cold by now, but, like the toast I'd ordered it's still lukewarm. Just like when I ordered them. The cafe owner had made the tea and the toast fresh, I'd watched him, but by the time I paid and made it to the table, both were lukewarm. Somehow, I'd guessed, the laws of physics don't work in this place. Time goes slower than anywhere else on earth. And heat dissipation is a nice theory that simply doesn't apply in here.

The noisy lads walk past my table on the way out, still as loud as when they came in. Still joking and jostling each other. I stare at the toast wondering if I'm ravenous enough to give it another try. The commotion the lads are causing gets louder and before I have a chance to look around, something splashes on me. On my face, my jacket, on my crisp white shirt. I'm drenched. Luckily, the cafes ineffective laws of physics mean I'm not scalded, but I am absolutely tea-stained soaked.

No one moves, no one talks, no one breathes. Everyone just stares at the once smart black girl who sits frozen and wet. Nothing seems real for those few seconds. Everything is surreal and dreamlike. Why else would this be happening to me?

'I'm so sorry,' the man who soaked me says, wrestling a handful of napkins from the metal napkin dispenser and trying to mop up his mess. He attempts to mop the drink from my face, gives up then tries my chest. Realising this is a bad idea, he goes for my face again. I snatch the soggy mound of brown and off-white paper from him and dare him to try and touch me again with a hard look.

'Looks like you scored there, Josh,' one of his friends say.

The final straw. In one move I scrape back my chair and stand up so fast, I knock the seat over. The lads, who'd been sniggering, stop when they realise I'm not like the girl behind the counter and I'm not going to put up with them.

'I'm sorry,' Josh says again. 'Is there anything I can do?'

'Yeh, go away,' I manage through my teeth. 'Now.'

Josh moves as though he wants to help me. Wants to do something. And for a moment I feel sorry him. Feel willing to accept his apology. But then I remember my interview. The job. My job. I scowl at him until he and his mates scuttle out of the cafe, leaving me with my soggy, stained clothes; my botched up make-up job and not a hope in hell of getting my job. Men. Fucking men. If they don't break your heart and leave you for dead, they ruin your life in another way. I pick up my chair then sink into it. Everyone's watching me, I can tell. But that's the least of my worries. There's no way out of this situation. I don't have time to go home. I'd only brought £10 out with me in case I had to hail a taxi, otherwise I'd left my purse and my cards at home – there was room in my bag for a notebook, my mobile and a pen. Nothing else. I cover my face with my hands and try to force myself to focus. How the hell am I going to get out of this one? What the hell am I going to do?

'May I join you?' someone asks.

It's him, Josh, Mr Life Wrecker. I'd recognise his voice anywhere. I can't speak to him, so I nod. What good will being nasty to him do? The deed is done now, there's little anyone can do about it.

'I really am sorry,' he says again.

I drag my hands down my face and stare vacantly at him. Not so long ago he would've been in a hospital bed with stitches all over his face. But now, after the last few months, when the fight has been knocked so severely out of me, I can do nothing but stare at him.

Were you going somewhere important?' he asks.

'Only to an interview for the job of my dreams,' I reply.

'Oh, God. I'll drive you home so you can get changed and drive you to your interview. My car isn't parked far from here.'

'It wouldn't be of any use. The rest of my wardrobe consists of T-shirts and jeans,' I say lying through my teeth. 'And there isn't time.' You must think I'm stupid as well as easy to drench, I thought. Drive off with a man who tried to drown me in tea and never be seen again? No, thank you very much.

'It's time I was going,' I say, despite having twenty-five minutes to go.

'Can't I have your phone number?' he asks suddenly.

'Sorry?'

'Your phone number. Can I have it?'

'Why?'

'To call you, of course.'

I size him up. He's all right looking if you like thin white guys with dark brown hair and navy blue eyes. I can't say I normally do. But I can appreciate the beauty in him. And maybe, I think as my eyes meet his, he could stir tings in me. Not much, but a little. All right, maybe he could stir tings in me a lot. However, that's not the point. 'Why would you want to ring me?'

'To see how your interview goes.'

'I can tell you now, how it'll go: 'Thanks but no thanks love. Have you seen the state of yourself, lately?''

'I'd still like to know how it went,' he replies.

'Why?'

'Because I'd like to get to know you.'

'Why?'

'Why do you ask so many questions? I only want your phone number.'

'I don't give my phone number to just anybody.'

'I'm not just anybody. I'm Josh Clarke.'

'Good for you,' I reply as I stand, grab my coat and bag.

'All right, here's my number. Call me later, we could go out for a drink. Or something to eat.' Josh holds out a business card.

I stare at him with something bordering on admiration. He really thinks I'll ring him. He doesn't for one second think I'll dash his card the second I get out of the door. I take his card, then make to leave.'Oh, good luck,' he says.

'Thanks,' I reply.

'I'll talk to you later then, Pretty Lady.'

'So you went?' My friend Betinna asks incredulously, when I tell her what happened later that day.

'Of course I went,' I replied. 'It woulda been rude not to show up. Never mind the fact they looked at me like I was some kind of ragamuffin who'd just walked in off the street.'

'Didn't you explain?'

'Of course I explained. And all they could see was me looking like some ragamuffin who'd walked in off the street.'

'This man who chucked the drink on you, is he a brother?'

'No.'

'And you're gonna see him?'

'I'm thinking about it.'

'You're mad girl.'

'The man ruined my life. He owes me.'

'He could be anybody, girl. He could do that all the time. For all you know he could be some mad killer who picks up his victims in cafes, murders dem, then buries their bodies where no one will ever find them.'

'You're being a bit dramatic aren't you?'

'Nah, man, you're crazy.

'What have I got to lose?'

'Your life, girl. Your life. You wouldn't catch me going out with some white guy I just met.'

'Well, you're not going out with him are you? I am.'

'You've gone right weird since you caught Jason messing with that girl. Men cheat, get over it, girl. Instead you never want to go out, or us girls to come round. We're yer mates. But the first white guy who asks you out, you just spread yer legs.'

'My mates? My girls? My mates woulda told me when they found out Jason was cheating.'

'We didn't know how to tell yer...'

'Yeh, right. You didn't tell me 'cause you wanted to have your titties on display to the whole world in the bridesmaid dress.'

Betinna's stunned silence is all I need to know that I've hit home. Hard. But I still felt bitter. She was my friend. We were meant to be share everything. Especially news that your man is laying more women than a farm of chickens lay eggs. And if she'd told me I wouldn't have walked in on Jason and the girl bumpin'n'grindin' to their own 'sweet music' on the floor of his recording studio, would I?

'You've lost it, girl,' Betinna says.

'That's the problem, I haven't,' I reply, suddenly realising what's wrong with me. I hang up on her without a goodbye. I've been living in an empty flat, going to work everyday and paying my bills, just like nothing had happened. Well all that's going to change. Because something has happened. Everything has happened. And I've got to do something about it.

Forty-five minutes later Josh turns the corner leading up to Leeds train station. He walks towards me with long purposeful strides.

In one hand he carries a briefcase, in the other his laptop computer. He looks perfectly unsuitable. Good. I could have sex with him and it wouldn't even matter, I say to myself. I could have a drink with him and it wouldn't even matter. Nothing would matter. Because I've got my job. Not *the* job. I'm sure I'll never hear from that lot again. But I've got my job. I called my editor before I called Josh. I was on a high. I was on a mission. I quit. The editor practically begged me to reconsider. Said they couldn't do without me. Said they'd been thinking of offering me a promotion and that I could have it. He even offered me lots more money. I said I would think about it. I wasn't playing hard to get, I really am going to think about it.

Jason and all my friends would say I'm stupid. They'd say that I should take what I'm offered and be grateful. Well two fingers to them. Two fingers to everyone who decided anything about my life. Everything, quitting, going out with Josh is terrifying. But it's what I want to do. Josh has nearly reached me now. We grin at each other across the short distance. Whether I see him again after tonight is immaterial. Whether I like him after tonight is immaterial. Because at last it's happened. At last I've become worthy. Worthy to live and enjoy my own life. And two fingers to anyone with a problem with that.

Author Notes

Glow Roger Robinson is a graduate of the infamous 'Speakers Corna' poetry jams at Brixton Art Gallery (from 1994 to 1996) and a former member of the now disbanded Urban Poets Society. He is currently the programmer for the Apples and Snakes performance poetry agency and has been chosen for the National Portrait Gallery's New Generation Poets Collection.

The Roaring Man Judith Bryan was born and raised in northwest London and worked as a social worker for a number of years. Her first novel *Bernard and the Cloth Monkey* won the 1997 Saga Prize and she has recently been awarded a New London Writers Award from the London Arts Board, to assist her in the writing of her second novel.

True Love Patricia Cumper graduated from Cambridge in 1976 and returned to her native Jamaica to write and produce two radio serials as well as write eight plays for which she won several national awards. She moved to Britain in 1993 and regularly writes drama for BBC radio. Her first novel, *One Bright Child*, was published in 1997.

The Great White Hate Courttia Newland is the author of the critically acclaimed novel *The Scholar* and the more recent *Society Within*. In his spare time he writes plays for a community based theatre project, The Post Office Theatre and short stories, which he hopes to publish in a collection of his own.

Joy Patsy Antoine is a freelance editor and journalist. She has worked in publishing for twelve years and was a judge for the 1997 Saga Prize. Joy is her first published short story.

Johnny Can Sleep Easy Now JJ Amoworo Wilson has had plays performed in Britain and southern Africa, and published short stories in various magazines. He has lived and worked in Egypt, Lesotho and Colombia and now teaches English as a Foreign language in London.

The Car Lucas Loblack was born in Shepherds Bush, London in 1967. In her late teens she studied business and finance and hotel management, but later had a change of direction and took a degree in Classical Studies at King's College London. She currently works in publishing and is working on her first novel.

Who Am I? Natalie Stewart has been performing on the London poetry scene since December 1998 and is known to many as the female connection in the 3 + 1 clique – the group having performed regularly at Urban Griots and Black Pepper. Having established herself as a well-respected poet Natalie is currently at work on her first novel.

The Price Of Maybe Kadija Sesay has edited two anthologies – *Six Plays by Black and Asian Women Writers* (1993), *Burning Words, Flaming Images* (1996), co-edited *IC3* and organises the Writer's HotSpot trips for writers. Her work in the creative arts has earned her a Cosmopolitan Woman of Achievement Award (1994) and a Candace Woman of Achievement Award (1996).

White Walls Deborah Ricketts has been writing poetry sporadically for a number of years. 'White Walls' is the first of her poems to be published.

Trust Me Brenda Emmanus is best known as presenter of The Clothes Show on BBC. She also regularly presents for both This Morning and Black Britain. 'Trust Me' is her first piece of published fiction.

Crates Joanna Traynor was the winner of the 1996 Saga Prize with her first novel *Sister Josephine*. Her second novel *Divine* has just been published and she's at work on her third.

A Good Buy Yinka Sunmonu is a freelance journalist and food columnist. She has written for numerous specialist publications including Community Care and Foster Care and has her own cookery column with National Bartender. She recently set up Novel Ideas, a company specialising in food promotions and events. She lives in Kent with her three children.

The Negative Norma Pollock was born in London in 1961 of Jamaican parentage. She is married and has worked for an inner city local authority for the past eleven years. In her spare time she has written many short stories and poems and has had three short stories published.

A Suitable Candidate Dorothy Koomson is a Leo, and proud of it. But she's even more proud of the fact that she's written and worked for many publications including New Woman, Pride, J17 and The Independent On Sunday. She was also runner-up in the 1998 Company Short Story Competition and writes erotic fiction for more! magazine (under a pseudonym, of course). Her unhealthy obsession with fiction writing began at 13 when she passed around her novels to her convent school classmates. She lives in London.